THE BARBARIAN WORLD

"I like you, Tanner," Rudo said. "You're the first savage I've met I could talk to." Hanging on the wall behind him were dark hanks of once-human hair.

"That's just as well, isn't it? But I'm not a true savage—not the kind you mean."

"No? You wear only a crude loinskin. You have only a scavenged knife, a bearskin, a deerskin, and a bare-breasted woman. . . . But you're not a savage, you say?"

I smiled. "Do I talk like one?"

"No. Why not? *Where do you come from, Tanner?*"

I couldn't tell him the truth: that I was part of what had destroyed civilization—that I was, in fact,

THE SPAWN OF THE DEATH MACHINE

The Spawn of the Death Machine

Ted White

WARNER
PAPERBACK
LIBRARY

A Warner Communications Company

WARNER PAPERBACK LIBRARY EDITION

First Printing: July, 1968
Second Printing: April, 1974

Cover illustration by A. Weston

for Rifka

Warner Paperback Library is a division of Warner Books, Inc.,
75 Rockefeller Plaza, New York, N.Y. 10019.

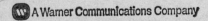 A Warner Communications Company

Printed in the United States of America

PROLOGUE

I was dreaming.

It was a place of darkness, lit only by a faint red spark. In my memory—how real?—that spark had been a deeper, more lustrous red, the rich red of flaming hair that wrapped itself protectively around me, as I had been enfolded in . . . *her* . . . arms.

The blackness was a gulf, a chasm, into which I endlessly fell, the spark a dying ember far away . . . above . . . and receding. I longed for . . . *her* . . . arms with an ache that instead of dwindling seemed to grow, spreading painfully throughout my limbs.

Then I was awake.

I hurt.

Every muscle in my body seemed to have its own distinctive ache. My skin was peppered—as if needles were lancing every square inch. I vibrated with racking pain.

After a while I tried opening my eyes. I closed them again. Dry steel wool was cemented to the undersides of my eyelids.

The needles were being pulled out; only the heat remained. It was soothing. I almost fell back into my black gulf of sleep. Then the heat receded, and I felt the chill metal surface hard under me. It was flat, cold, and uncomfortable. My shoulder blades dug against its hard surface.

I opened my eyes again.

The light was a deep blue, flickering at the edge of my vision. Near ultraviolet.

I turned my head to my right.

A blank metal wall, highlights on its dull polished surface resonating to the violet glow—only inches beyond my right shoulder.

My neck was stiff and felt as if someone had been holding it in a hammerlock. But I turned my head the other way.

Another metal wall. Further away, this time. And, closer, the edge of the surface upon which I was lying. A shelf? Metal, like everything else in this cell.

It's uncomfortable, lying flat on a metal shelf. Without pausing to check my body's willingness, I sat up, swinging my legs around and off the shelf.

My toes grazed the floor. Shrugging, I stood up.

The cell was seven feet high and seven feet long. The shelf upon which I'd been lying was three feet wide, and jutted straight out from the wall on its side. The space in which I now stood was another three feet wide.

An absolutely featureless, metal-walled cell, seven feet by seven feet by six feet, and filled with the glow of near-ultraviolet light. No doors, no windows. I was completely contained. I was trapped.

Claustrophobia closed down on me with sudden impact. For a moment I felt the walls actually growing closer.

I'd been put through a machine; pummelled, maybe tortured. But when I examined my naked body, there were no scars, bruises, or any signs of physical abuse. It puzzled me.

I stopped and peered under the metal shelf. The violet glow penetrated well enough for me to see a thin slot just below the place where the shelf joined the wall. I put my hand to it. Fresh air kissed my skin.

The closeness of the stale air was only an illusion. My quickening breath was a purely psychological reaction.

A metal cell: what did it mean? How had I been put here? And why?

No facilities for eating; no sanitation. Just fresh air. Why?

"*Tanner!*"

The voice reverberated deafeningly in the tiny room.

Tanner? Who? Me?

I grunted.

"*Tanner, listen. You have been asleep for a long time. You've been in the cold sleep.*"

"Yeah?" I said. My voice was rusty in my throat. "I don't remember."

"*That is not necessary.*" The voice spoke coldly. Its

inflections were as metallic as the cell walls. *"You have been awakened for a new purpose."*

"You," I said. "Who are you?"

"This is the Com-Comp. Your creator."

"I don't believe that."

"You are an artificially constructed human being, a mobile data-gathering device."

There was no point in trying to contradict the voice. I didn't know.

"It has become necessary to gather fresh data. You have been reactivated in order to seek out new and relevant data."

"Meaning——?"

"These are your instructions: You will go out into the world of Man for the period of one year. In that year, you will accumulate a true knowledge of the present state of humanity in the outside world. At the end of one year, you will return here."

My pulse quickened. Outside——! It evoked no images for me, but somewhere something stirred in my slumbering unconscious. More immediately, it meant escape from this barren cell. "How will I know what's relevant data for you?" I asked.

"Everything you accumulate in your memory banks will be relevant," the Com-Comp said. *"Your memories have been wiped clean of prior knowledge. When you return, data retrieval will be one hundred per cent."*

"All right," I said. "When do I start?"

"Now."

The long wall at my side suddenly slid back, revealing a doorway three feet wide. Beyond was a narrow hallway, lit by the same violet glow. I stepped through.

The air smelled long-confined and dead. There was an antiseptic cleanliness, an absence of dust or even mustiness. Like distilled water, the air was chemically pure, but inert.

The hall stopped at a metal-runged ladder that climbed a vertical shaft. There was nothing else to do, nowhere else to go. I started climbing.

I climbed at least sixty feet before the shaft ended and I stepped out upon a landing. As I did, the wall at the far end slid back, and a minor deluge of earth, sod, and shrubbery fell in. The odor of crushed leaf-mold was pungent in my nostrils, and the sudden bright shaft of yellow sunlight wrenched at my eyes.

As I knuckled the tears from my eyes I heard a second panel slide shut behind me. I was cut off from the stairs and the cell below. I felt no loss.

I drew several deep breaths of fresh air, picking out a multitude of scents which I could not then identify, but which smelled rich and satisfying. There came a scrabbling sound at my feet. I looked down. Tiny metal tentacles had darted out from the base of the walls. Wherever they touched the broken clods of dirt, the metal floor was instantly clean again.

It came to me very forcefully then that I did not want to stand upon this dead metal floor any longer. I no longer wanted to breathe canned air, nor have my eyes assailed by the marginal flicker of violet light. Beyond the ragged opening stood the outside world. I needed no more urging to enter it.

PART ONE

CHAPTER ONE

Tall trees stood sentinel around the hillock from which I emerged. Coarse grass sawed at my ankles. Ahead of me, tangled wilderness. Behind me, a raw scar of fresh dirt and gleaming metal. The portal was closed. I stood alone, naked, defenseless, in a world about which I knew nothing.

What was I supposed to do? *Go out into the world for the period of one year?* I was there. *Accumulate a true knowledge of the present state of humanity . . . ?* What humanity?

The sun was almost uncomfortably warm on my bare skin. I caught the distant keening of insects on the sluggish breeze. Overhead fluffy banks of warm white clouds drifted against a hazy blue sky. The underbrush thinned under the tall close trees.

I found a narrow meandering trail, and followed it through the forest. It paused by a narrow brook and then climbed across a naked outcropping of worn rock.

I almost missed the fire hydrant.

It was chipped almost free of its paint, and the metal was pitted and rusty. It was the color of a tree-stump. *Fire hydrant.* I was staring at this obviously human artifact, and the two words came reflectively to my tongue. "Fire hydrant," I said aloud. Then, "But, what's a 'fire hydrant'?"

I didn't know. I *felt* I knew, but nothing followed those two words. No explanation rose to the bidding of my conscious mind.

Short, squat, a truncated cross that was half-eaten by corrosion: *fire hydrant:* human artifact—half buried by leaves in what seemed otherwise virgin forest. I shook my head and left it behind me.

The trees began thinning. Then, abruptly, they were gone.

9

I faced the fallen ruins of a city.

Grass and creepers covered the wide open place between the trees and the ruins. Beyond, skeletons of stone fought free of their verdant bondage to point empty fingers at the sky.

Manhattan, I thought. *New York City.*

And then, again, I wondered why.

"*Your memories have been wiped clean of prior knowledge,*" the Com-Comp had said. But obviously not completely. I knew enough to talk and to understand what I was told. I knew enough to use my body as I must once have learned to do—walking, climbing, running.

And odd, unknown words kept returning to me. Words: labels: meaningless beyond their obvious connotations. Symbols of another time, and another memory.

I had seen this city once before, then.

It felt as though that must have been a long, long time before.

I prowled the ruins until sundown without flushing anything bigger than a furred animal the size of my forearm. This must once have been a vast city, for its ruins stretched on as far as the eye could see.

Dusk brought with it strange pangs in my midsection, and the urge to find shelter for the night. The dimming light did not seem in itself sufficient reason to stop my explorations, but my limbs ached, the soles of my feet were sore, and from somewhere I recalled the vestiges of a dream.

It would be nice to sleep and find that dream again.

I found a basket of vines in a niche-like building corner, and wormed my way into them. Then I closed my eyes on my first day, and fell easily asleep.

It took me six days to establish that these were indeed the ruins of a vast city—and that as far as humans went, they were quite unpopulated.

I also discovered *hunger.* It did not come upon me immediately, but on the fifth day it was a pervading ache that filled my midsection. When the first cramp hit me, I doubled up as though from a blow, and fell to my knees. It was then that the strange thought came to me: *I am hungry. I must eat.* And immediately I remembered . . .

10

I remembered with a fullness, a depth and breadth of associated senses so rich that I was dizzied. Sitting in a *chair,* before a *table,* the still-sizzling *steak* wafting its odors of *rare, singed beef, brushed with garlic.* It was in a room of delicate golden illumination. My *sleeve* brushed through the *salad* to my right, picking up some of its *cheese dressing.* It annoyed me, and I spoke . . . to someone . . .

It was gone. That was all there was of it: that and no more. I had, encapsulated, one tiny fragment of my past life, meaningless in terms of the life I'd once lived, perhaps, but enormously rich in suggestions. I found my mouth full of saliva at the remembered odors, while my consciousness struggled with those subtler remnants. *Clothing.* I remembered the feel of the clothing draped around and fastened to my body, and suddenly I felt naked—naked as I'd not felt at any moment before. I was unprotected.

Another cramp struck me, and that brought me back again to my real problem: hunger.

What did I eat?

Somehow I knew, without needing explanations, that a meal of *steak and salad* was a processed sort of food. I could not expect to find it here, in the wilderness.

Meat came from animals.

I was fairly certain of that. Therefore, it followed: catch an animal.

I caught an animal. It was about the length of my forearm, its fur striped in shades of tan and white, its tail suddenly puffed to twice its normal thickness when it saw me.

I'd seen its tracks in the dust, and climbed to a crumbling ledge overhead, where I'd lain prone in wait.

The sun was low on the horizon and the rubble-filled once-street below was heavy with shadow when the animal came skulking out of the vines, sniffed around suspiciously, turned, looked up, and saw me.

Time seemed to freeze.

We stared into each other's eyes, the animal and I, and I saw that it understood. I was hungry. It was food. Its ears laid back on its head, its back arched, and its tail fur seemed to swell out. I saw all of this even as I struggled up-

11

ward, against a strange great weight, flinging myself up and off the ledge.

Very slowly, almost as in a dream, I fell for the animal, which seemed unable to move. My feet struck the dust, my knees buckled, and I was straightening when, lazily, the creature made a hissing noise and began rearing back, humping its back impossibly, its forearms still outstretched before it, claws extended.

I felt my pulse hammering great ponderous throbs at my temples as I strained forward, thrusting my hands through liquid air at the animal.

It squirmed with a rippling violence. It seized my left wrist with its teeth, then its claws were raking at my left forearm, its hind feet kicking my hand and tearing away strips of my skin.

But my left hand was at its neck. With my right hand, I grabbed its head. I twisted.

A snap. Then it was limp.

I dropped it back into the dust and stared at my left hand and arm.

Blood welled from the long slashes on my forearm, from the chunk bitten from the side of my thumb, from the lacerations in the heel of my palm and the outside of my wrist. It was a darkening red, and for a moment I let it drip off the ends of my fingers. My hand hurt.

Somehow, this seemed altogether wrong. I lifted my arm, and examined it. The blood was thicker now. It was no longer flowing out unchecked. And it was darker. Even in a nearby patch of rust sunlight, it was blackening.

But nonetheless, I felt much less hungry.

CHAPTER TWO

Later that night, when my hand felt only numb and no longer hurt, I ate the animal. I ate it raw, and I ate some of its fur. It did not taste very good—nothing like my single memory of other food—and I did not enjoy the experience. But the cramps left my stomach, and the feeling of satiation was satisfying.

It was clear to me, however, that this was a wholly unsatisfactory way to eat. It didn't make sense to chance wounding or maiming myself for another meal as unpleasant as this one.

The next morning, when I awoke to the brightness of day, a more pleasant surprise awaited me.

My hand had healed. The scabs had fallen away from the claw cuts and slashes, leaving bright pink skin. The side of my thumb was still crusted with dried blood, and itched interminably, but seemed better. I could move and flex my hand, and the only pain was a sort of dull ache when I strained against the crust of my remaining wound.

Perhaps this hunting for one's food was not such a bad sort of thing after all. I'd gone five days before needing to do it before; in another five days I'd probably not mind doing it again.

I was on a peninsula, or perhaps an island; it was hard to tell. But I'd established the fact that from the place where I'd first entered the ruins, they progressed southward without pause until the land met water.

To the east across a stretch of water I could see tiered terraces and more ruins. There were also abutments which suggested bridges, but none stood. To the west was a wider stretch of water, and, on the opposite shore, yet more empty-looking ruins. To the south, water. Only the north offered any hope.

Not once had I come upon even the suggestion of human life. Animal life I'd found in fair abundance—although most if it, to judge by the tracks and glimpses I'd had, was no larger than the creature I'd caught and eaten. Birds were plentiful. But the narrow trails through the underbrush and the rubble were the hunting trails of small animals, and I found not one single sign of human presence.

I ventured into the subterranean depths of the ruined city only once—on the sixth day.

I was returning slowly north, this time along the eastern side of the island. I'd found a relatively wide and open boulevard and I was making better time than usual. The sun was hot on my back, and my feet scuffed up dust that hung in little clouds in the still air before settling behind me. The ruins were all brightness and shadow, very stark in the morning light.

To my left, I saw an open hole in the street. Stairs led down into the darkness.

Could it be that humans might live *below* the ground, I wondered?

The rubble that was strewn upon the steps seemed to belie that notion, but still I was intrigued. An obviously inviting set of steps that led down into the underground: who could resist?

Cool air closed in around me with the smell of dampness.

Light seemed at first a problem, but when my eyes adjusted to the gloom I saw that the sun penetrated in thin fingers through cracks and holes in the pavement above. Some of the openings seemed so even and regular that they must have been planned so.

At the bottom of the steps was a vestibule. A metal fence separated this from a shadowy area beyond. I gave the fence a push, and it collapsed. My hand was covered with a thick red-brown powder that had flaked off at my touch. The fence crashed to the floor with many echoes, and then, as these sounds died, the air was filled with frantic scampering animal sounds. Retreating . . .

The area beyond was much darker, and the air seemed caught and close, the scent of organic decay carried on clammy tendrils. I followed a bend in the wall, and suddenly the dank darkness clamped down on me like a physical enwrapment. I had to glance back over my shoulder to see the patch of lighter grey that told me from whence I'd come; claustrophobia gripped me.

I stepped on something that *squished*.

Immediately a fetid stench rose into the air, and the taste

14

of bile filled my mouth. My foot felt smeared with slime.

Patter . . . patter. . . . Drawing nearer.

My reaction was purely instinct. I jumped.

And fell five feet. I hit on my right foot on something long and narrow, my foot, still coated with slime, slipping and twisting out from under me. I caught myself with my hands and knees, sudden pain lancing up from my ankle. It wasn't until I'd sat and regained my breath that I realized my left hand was hurting again too—I'd torn open my wound.

I was sitting in a shallow stream of water. Something warm breathed on my leg.

I shouted, in sudden panic, "*No!* Go, go!"

Pitter-pitter-pitter-pitter . . . Retreating, again.

Whatever it was could be no more startled than I was myself. But the sound of my voice gave me a sudden comfort too. It told me I was here, in a real place, and had at least myself for company.

Crash! It sounded far away, but with so many echoes, who could be sure?

I stood up and began groping in the dark. There: a patch of grey. And here: my hands found the edge over which I'd tumbled. My ankle protested, my hand protested, but they both helped me up, onto the higher surface, without malingering.

And I straightaway made for that patch of grey light.

When I rounded the corner and saw thin bars of real sunlight, golden ingots in the gloom, it was like seeing an old, long-forsaken friend.

I hobbled up the stairs with every bit of speed I could manage. And I sat on the topmost step, just soaking up the high noon heat, like a man warming himself before the fire. I needed no more confirmation. Humans might've built that subterranean chamber, but they surely lived there no longer.

To my surprise, the ruins surrounded the forest from which I'd first emerged, at least on the east. As I followed mile after mile of them, I pushed steadily northward until once more I came to water.

But this was a narrow river that seemed sluggish and without much current. On the other side the land rose in higher folds of hills studded with the green of regrown forest, through which the ruins sent infrequent yellowed teeth.

The sun was already low behind me, high enough yet to paint the hills to the northeast with broad swashes of warm yellows, but sunk beneath my sight behind a ridge to the west. Night would be falling soon. But quite suddenly I knew with great certainty that I did not wish to spend another night in these ruins. My experience underground had sobered me; it had made this trek of exploration less of a light-hearted sort of adventure.

There seemed to be but one way to cross the river: I must swim it.

I crossed great stretches of concrete, thin grasses poking timidly from spidering cracks, and climbed a low barricade. Then I was at a wall, staring down into the water.

It was twelve, perhaps fifteen feet down. The water was dark, unclear, uninviting. Its surface had a greasy sheen. It lapped at the stone wall with a lazy *thlepp . . . thlepp. . . .* The stones near the waterline were dark with moss. It seemed I stood there, staring down, for a long time.

At last I turned and lowered myself, face to the wall, feet probing for toe-holds in the wall, until I was hanging by my fingers. Thus committed, I had no direction to go but down. Kicking the wall with my feet, I let go, flinging out my arms and thrusting myself out and backward, away from the wall.

It's just as well I did. I hit with a shallow back-dive that stung my back and shoulders with the slap of the water, but as I shook the water from my face and peddled my feet under me, my toes touched the slippery, uneven surfaces of jagged rocks no more than five feet under the surface. If I'd dived or jumped straight down, I'd almost certainly have hit those rocks, and hard.

The water smelled brackish, like dead fish and dilute salt, and I held my face up out of the water as best I could as I swam. Like walking, swimming seemed to come instinctively to me. I must have done it before, but no memories returned to guide me. I simply swam, kicking my legs and throwing one arm after the other to pull me through the water. It was tiring and it was monotonous. I did it until I reached the opposite shore. Then I climbed

16

out as weary as I'd been since this whole thing had begun.

I blundered through the gloom of dusk to the first copse of trees, then collapsed on the soft bed of dead pine needles beneath them. Sleep came instantly.

At first I thought it was my Dream again. A pale face, dark hair re-silvered at the edges by the moon it eclipsed, hung close over me, wide eyes staring down at me. Her breath fell warmly upon my cheek. Then the face suddenly receded, and the full moon filled my vision, its cool clean light washing all else into deep shadow.

"He look young," she breathed. Her voice was scented with roses, a thorny huskiness that caught in her throat.

"Best we kill him," spoke a male voice. It was rubble, grinding.

I sat bolt upright. My eyes were already open. Four men stood in front of me, the girl to one side. They were all rough silhouettes in the shadowed moonlight. I blinked away the indistinctness and saw that they were clothed in rough leathers and furs that girded only their torsos and lower legs and feet. They wore beards, and their hair was shoulder-length, little shorter than the girl's. Three held long sharpened staves of wood. All three were pointed at me: at my chest. The fourth was the one who had spoken.

"Kill me?" I asked. "Why?"

A frown clouded his brow. His chest rumbled. "Don't need you," he said, finally. "Need women. Not you."

"He's got no beard," one of the others said, his voice thin and reedy.

Another laughed. "Half woman, he is!" He pointed with his spear.

The girl wrapped her arms about herself and stepped further back.

Warily, I eased up onto my feet, first to a crouch, then standing. Something sharp nudged my back.

"Maybe we shouldn't kill him right away," a voice said behind me.

I looked back at the one who'd first spoken. I could see now that his hair and beard were edged with grey. I'd taken it for a trick of the moonlight. He seemed to be the spokesman. He nodded. "Not yet," he agreed. He inclined his head.

Immediately, three spear-points, only one of which was within my range of vision, nudged me in the direction he'd indicated. I turned and followed.

They led me only a short distance to their "village."

It was a sad, pitiable excuse for any village deserving that name. Its odor marked its presence before I could see it. And when I saw it, at first I did not realize it.

A great concrete slab was tilted at an angle, a stout tree having grown up under it to edge it into the air and support it. The ground under the slab had been burrowed out a little. Ragged skins hung from its edge to make tent-walls. In front of it was a clearing of trampled bare earth. To one side a cooking fire smouldered.

I was pitched forward into the center of the bare area. The men—there were eight of them—did a lot of laughing, and a couple slapped my buttocks. I landed on my hands, and remained in a crouch, turning to watch the ringleader.

The girl had trailed along behind. Two more women came out from under the slab, pushing the skins aside. One of them, scrawny but obviously wiry, seized the girl roughly. "Where you been?"

The girl said nothing, but the gravel-voiced one threw back his head and laughed. The older woman growled, but said nothing.

"We brung back food," one of the younger men said, apparently in an effort to mollify the woman.

"Bet you did," she said, harshly. "Sneak out a-sporting, and tumble some game, didja? You take whole lot of 'em with ya so it won't get away? Big man!" She laughed. She didn't seem amused.

"Aw, now," he said, his voice smaller, less rumbling than before. "On this buck we kin feast a week."

It was slow getting to me. I don't think it had come home to me what they were talking about until that very point. And that's the moment when someone clouted me, and I went back into a painful sleep.

CHAPTER THREE

It was daylight again when I awoke. I ached in several unusual places. My head was throbbing quite unpleasantly. My wrists were tied behind me, and my ankles bound. I was lying on my side.

A fist descended over my face and entangled itself in my hair. With a jolt that snapped my chin back, I was yanked to my knees by my hair. A grizzled, bearded face lowered itself level with mine, and the stench of rotten breath clogged my nostrils.

I threw up all over him.

He dropped me, and I fell against the ground. My limbs were numb, and my shoulder had no feeling when I landed on it. He did a lot of cursing, and wiped his hand across his face and at me. I wished my own hand was free; tears distorted my vision.

I was left alone for a while after that, and in that time I had the chance to size up the campsite a little better.

The dwelling was, as I said, basically an uptilted slab with walls of hanging animal skins—none of them large; they were pieced together crudely—with a bare stretch of earth for a front porch. Trees ringed the clearing. As I watched, a squat, ugly woman—only the third I'd seen here—hunkered down under a tree, lifted her skirt of skins, and defecated. The spot she chose, as I could see from the buzzing swarms of flies, was popular, but far from the only one in sight. That accounted for the foul odor which hung over the place. These people seemed to have absolutely no interest in their own sanitation.

The girl crossed into my line of vision. In broad daylight I could see she was not as attractive as I'd found her in my semi-awakened state the night before. Her hair *was* red, a flaming red that caught the shafts of sunlight and spun them into sparks of living fire, and that seemed to touch something locked deep within me. But, like the other two women in this group, she had a sallow, undernourished look to her. Her face was filthy, but her eyes seemed ringed by darker circles. She was bare above the waist, like the other women, and her breasts were small. Below them her

19

ribs stood out. Her arms and legs were covered with the long dotted lines of scratch scabs, apparently from the underbrush. Her knees were scarred and dirty. She wore a short skirt of skins, and brief skin-coverings on her feet. She looked bored, tired, unhappy, and restless, and she seemed careful never to look quite at me. I wondered why my gaze kept returning to her.

I was lying under the tree that held up the slab-roof of the dwelling. I was facing outward, only a corner of the slab caught within my eyesight. The tree seemed curiously scarred and bent where it supported the slab, and the concrete of the slab was the same orange-rust color I'd seen so often in the ruins across the river. When I looked closely, I could see exposed rods of metal at the edges, and make out the pebbly texture of the uneven surface of the slab.

A bright red bird settled on a branch overhead, and sang a little song. Something wet struck my back and dribbled across my shoulders to the ground. A furry little animal ran across a limb, and the bird leapt, flustered, into the air. The furry animal made angry, *chirring* noises. It was a very peaceful morning.

I wondered what was going to happen to me. I'd been caught and made captive without hardly a fight, and if I had anyone to blame it could only be myself. I was naive, stupid, to have thought that if I found humans they would welcome me easily into their company.

It would appear I was considered game. Food. To be caught and eaten as easily as I'd caught and eaten my own prey. I did not like the idea.

There were noises in the dwelling behind me. They had been going on for some time: gruff, grunting noises, irregularly rhythmical. I had ignored them, since they seemed a part of the background of noises about me.

The red-haired girl seemed unwilling to approach the dwelling. She seemed to be at a loss for something to do. I caught myself wishing she would look at me; I wanted to catch her eye.

Suddenly there was a shrill shriek of pain, answered almost immediately by the sound of flesh striking flesh, and a hoarse guttural exclamation. Red-head looked up. Her face was frightened. She exchanged looks with the squat woman at the fire. She began moving carefully toward the trees.

20

A flap of skin slapped against me, and the skinny woman scrambled over me, running across the clearing. She was as naked as I was.

Something kicked me in the small of my back and catapulted me outward from under the tree. I rolled, then felt a heavy weight slam down across my back, grinding my face in the dirt.

Curses exploded above me. Hands seized me and pulled me up to my feet. It was him again: old Grizzly. I saw his open hand sweep out, and I tried to duck. I was too stiff, too awkward. The blow caught my left ear, and knocked me to the ground again. I rolled and his kick just missed my face.

The bastard had stumbled over me and fallen flat. Was that his fault, for leaving me tied up there in his way? It was not. It was mine, for being there. And since the first victim of his rage had already disappeared among the trees, the others had also ducked from sight, and I was all that was left, I was It. He was shrieking and rumbling with exploding anger, his voice an inarticulate jumble of snuffings and snorts, his eyes wide, mouth wide, nostrils distended, spittal in his beard, his midsection bare, and his genitals covered with the glistening slime of a rutting animal. He came at me.

I rolled again, backwards, and onto my knees.

His still-booted foot lashed out, caught me under my jaw, and nearly tore my head from my shoulders, smashing my teeth together, lifting my body from the ground, and filling my vision with pure white light.

My nose was full of the stench of him. My body was being torn apart by him. And my heart was filling with simmering rage. It was an experience new to me.

I did not feel a thing as I tore the leather thongs free of my wrists. I saw the bracelets of blood that banded them when I swung my arms around in front of me, but I felt no pain.

I felt no pain anywhere. I was floating, slowly, in a world of bright light and sharp vision, but muted sounds and smothered motion. I pushed myself forward, bending down, and hooked my fingers on the thongs that bound my ankles. I saw the blood ooze around my fingers as the leather tore into them, saw the flesh rip from my legs as the bonds tore free. Something caught the sun on my right wrist and gleamed silver through the blood for a moment.

Then, still swimming through air as thick as water, I came to my feet, fully freed.

Grizzly seemed paralyzed, his mouth open and working, but terribly slowly. His arms were wide outspread, as though to welcome me in an embrace against his hairy chest.

I drove my right hand, fingers outstretched and stiff, under his ribcage on his left side. It was like plunging my hand through a thin skin into something soft and fiery.

His eyes protruded, and then his tongue was caught in his open mouth. His face darkened, violently. He was dead, although not yet aware of it. I pulled back, my right hand crimson, while his useless guts spilled out from him. His heart was already ruptured.

Time seemed to return to normal then, and he crumpled into a heap less than half the size he'd been while living, and fell soundlessly to the bare ground.

I went over to another tree and was sick again.

The red-headed girl approached me hesitantly. I was sitting in the dust. My body felt like one large wound. The sun beat down upon me, and I was in the center of a furnace that seemed to swirl around me. I was light-headed, giddy almost, my face very hot, very dry.

"Take me with you?"

I looked up at her. She was a thin blur. "Take you . . . where?" I mumbled.

"Away. Anywhere."

I shook my head. The movement gave me vertigo, and it was hard for me to concentrate. "Dunno," I said. "Dunno if I'm going . . . anywhere . . ."

"You killed him," she said.

"Uh-huh."

"When the others get back, they'll kill you. They will. Uuna ran off for them. She'll find them. She'll bring them back. You got to run."

"Uuna?"

"His wife. His first one, I mean. The old one."

Both the other two women seemed of an equal age. But I managed to focus on the dead man, and the squat ugly

22

woman was methodically pulling his boots off. So she wasn't Uuna.

The girl followed my gaze, looked startled for a moment, then ducked behind me, into the dwelling. I blinked, and she was back, a mess of smelly skins in her hands.

The squat one hunkered down in front of me and grinned. Most of her teeth were missing. She held the boots out to me.

"Your boots," she said. Her voice was surprisingly soft.

"Your clothes," the girl added, holding the skins.

To the victor went the spoils.

"You got any water?" I asked.

The girl dropped the skins in the dust and jumped up. It hurt my eyes to follow her quick movements. I heard the skins fall shut behind her, then rustle aside again, and again she was back. She was an eager young thing.

She held a bottle. It was of glass, peculiarly purpled in a mottled effect along one side and part of another. The remainder was clear. The water was not. But I did not pause to reflect on this sad fact. I took it from her with hands that shook and tremblingly raised to it to my lips. I drank a good bit.

Then I splashed some on my face, and poured the rest over my body. It washed off a little dust, but not much else. My odor was an offense to my own nostrils.

I was caked with blood, mud, the remains of my two-day-old meal, bits of Grizzly, and a few miscellanea. But I wasn't bleeding any more, and although I was still feverish, I did feel a little better. My eyes seemed to stay in focus.

"Okay," I said. I nodded at the other woman. "You too?"

"Huh?"

"You coming too?"

"No," she said, her voice sad. "I stay. Uuna and me—we better off here. You go. Better soon."

The girl picked up the boots and pushed them on my feet. I didn't stop her. She helped me to my feet. Then she wrapped the skins round my waist and fastened them. They made a crude skirt, not unlike her own. It seemed to pass for clothes. It felt hot, close, greasy, and uncomfortable. I left it on.

I saw no weapons lying about. I didn't feel like poking

23

behind the skins under the slab.

"Which way the others go?" I asked.

The girl pointed down the hill towards the river.

"Okay," I said, and took her hand, leading the way up through the trees towards the crest of the hill.

The boots helped. And the skirt too. The way was rugged, climbing over jumbles of stone and jagged chunks of concrete, pushing through brambly underbrush, fighting our way through thickets that clutched and tore at us. My feet had become toughened among the ruins, but the leather of the boots, already scarred, gained fresh cuts that might as easily have been in my skin. And while my legs and chest and back quickly became a mass of thin scratches, I appreciated the fact that my more tender parts were spared.

But I hoped to find a fresh stream soon.

When we were over the first hill and crossing a valley thick with ruins, I asked the girl, "What's your name?" The question seemed to startle her, and her grip on my hand tightened convulsively, but she answered quickly.

"Rifka," she answered.

A vague disappointment touched me, then passed. I tried to pursue it, internally. Why had I felt that? What had I wanted? Whose name did I want to hear?

"I'm Tanner," I said. It seemed to satisfy her. She didn't let go. She hadn't let go once. Her palm was small, moist, and callused. It felt nice in mine.

"You know this way?" I asked. "You been here before?"

"No," she said. Her voice was small and tense. "Never. I never come here."

"Why?"

We were climbing over a heap of rubble between the ruins of two buildings. Trees grew inside their walls.

She gestured with her free hand. "All this. The Old Places . . . they aren't safe, sometimes."

"How do you know?"

"I just know." She paused, as if seeking a better answer. "Everybody knows."

"I guess it's a pretty safe way to come, then. They won't follow us here, I mean."

24

"Yeah," she said. "I guess they won't."

I was tired. Even coming this short distance had exhausted me. "Let's sit for a bit," I said. I found a bench-like flat slab and eased down on it, releasing her hand. She hesitated, then sat beside me. She seemed nervous, or scared.

"Rifka," I said. The sound of her name jerked her head around. "Do I scare you?"

"You? No. I mean, I dunno. Maybe."

"What scares you?"

"This," she said, waving her hand at the surrounding ruins. They were a river, running through the narrow valley. "Here. I don't like it here."

"That scares you most?"

"Yeah."

"What about me scares you?"

"You? You *fast*. What you did to Poll. So *fast*." She was staring at her lap, her arms hugging her chest.

"Fast? What do you mean?"

"You—you just *lying* there. Then there's blood. Blood on your arms, and blood on your legs, and you untied. Then——" She clapped her hands together. The sound was loud in the silence of the ruins. "Then you kill Poll. That fast. I couldn't see. Just you on the ground, then you standing. And Poll dead. He dinna see either." She paused in the sudden rush of her words. "Strong. You strong, too. You break loose. You kill Poll with one hand." She shook her head, eyes downcast.

"Why'd you want to come with me, then?" I asked. I stared at my wrists. The blood was caked in thick scabs around them. I had little memory of ripping the leather thongs free. That hadn't been me.

"To get away," Rifka said.

"Tell me about yourself," I suggested. "Why'd you want to run away?"

So, in short sentences, in broken grammar, Rifka explained. She paused often, hesitating to believe that I could want to hear her. For her it was probably the longest speech of her life. The words did not come easily. Her vocabulary seemed very limited.

"Poll kill my people," she began. "He kill Papa-Semm, Karl, Daul, Semmell, Mox. He take me, Mama-Ilke.

25

Mama-Ilke, she try to bite this thing off, he hit her, kill her."

Basically, these people lived in tribes. They were loose family units, living a nomadic life as hunters. Women were scarce, and prized. Men were common, and those of another family were fair game. Rifka had been young. She made a gesture that indicated it had been before her hips had swelled and her breasts had started: pre-puberty—when Poll's tribe had surprised and killed hers. Her father and brothers had been taken as game, she and her mother captured for the tribe. Her mother had lasted a single day.

Humans were considered better game than any of the other animals that frequented the area. Rifka herself had shared the piecemeal consumption of her former family. Once adopted in her new tribe, she was highly prized. She was young, and not unattractive. She got along.

Poll wasn't her first. Her own father had claimed that honor, and her brothers had soon followed the trail he'd blazed. She expected little better of Poll and his sons, and was not surprised.

That had been maybe three years ago, she said.

I revised my estimate of her age downwards. Fifteen, possibly sixteen years old. She seemed both very young and very old. I wondered what to do with her.

"What am I to do with you?" I asked.

She seemed honestly puzzled.

"I mean, I'm not going to stay around here," I said.

"Where you going?"

I shrugged; my shoulders ached. "I don't know. But away. Away from here."

"Take me with you."

"Why?"

"I don't like it here," she said, simply.

Well, that made sense.

CHAPTER FOUR

The countryside was folded into great furrows, ruins choking their depths, fresh growth green upon their crests. We followed a ridge northward. Rifka said only the Great Ruins and water lay to the south.

The going was not easy for me. Rifka marveled that I managed to move at all. I'd found a stream of clear, fresh water, and I'd bathed in it. My skin felt better for losing its patina of blood and dirt, and although my ankle and wrist wounds began bleeding again, I was certain they were cleansed.

Before donning my clothes again, I washed and pounded them by the side of the stream. This seemed to confuse the girl.

"Why you do that?"

I dunked the skins that had wrapped my loins in the gentle current. Several small insects squirmed free of the folds and seams, and were swept away by the water. I pointed at them, without saying anything. Then I rubbed the skins in the sand in the shallows where I squatted. After I'd done this two or three times, rinsing each time, I laid the broad skirt out on a flat rock, and, after hunting briefly for one, began scraping it with a sharp-edge rock. I scraped both sides while the sun beat down upon my back, drying and tightening the skin across my shoulder blades, and Rifka looked stolidly on. Her expression said I was a little crazy. But obviously, it helped to be crazy.

I rubbed the skins with sand again, and rinsed them a final time. I did not try to explain my actions. I could not have explained them. I only had a *feeling*—that nagging impression from somewhere beneath my consciousness— that this would clean the leather skins.

And I was right.

While the skirt dried in the sun, I worked over the boots. With these I had to be more gentle. They were crudely made, of leather wrapped around itself and fastened with thongs. I had to be careful they didn't fall apart. I contented myself with a thorough immersion—which dislodged a small swarm of desperately swimming bugs—and some pounding with the back edge of the rock. Then, the boots also displayed limply for the sun, I turned to Rifka.

"Now, you," I said.

She drew back. Her boredom turned suddenly to fear.

"What, me?" she asked. I noticed her teeth were yellowed.

"It's time to clean you up," I said, gesturing at the stream.

She shook her head violently. "No, no. Not me. No."

I took her arm, gently, at the wrist. "Yes," I said. "We've got to get you clean."

She showed no liking for the idea. Her eyes were very wide, darting and searching from side to side. She plainly wanted to scream, but was afraid to. She raised her free arm and began pummeling me with her fist.

I tried to catch at the thong that held her skirt, but she kept twisting her body and raining her angry little blows on me.

"Look, Rifka," I said. "Stop this. *Stop,* I say!" I might as well have been talking to a tree.

She was starting to kick at me now, and she was no longer making a fist with her open hand. Once her nails clawed my chest, and then an unfortunate kick hit my left ankle where I'd ripped the thongs free.

Right then, I decided to stop playing this silly game. Reflexively my grip tightened on her wrist, and she made a little mew of pain. Then I had my other hand on her thigh, and I lifted her off the ground.

I didn't try to hold her. That would have hurt her more. Instead, I let her body momentum swing her back and then I pitched her forward—out into the stream.

She landed with a splash on her back and a large yelp. She tried to get her feet under her to stand, but I'd deliberately thrown her into the center of the stream where it was deepest, for fear of letting her hit the rocks in the shallow area, and the current was too strong for her. She pitched and staggered, slipping and floundering, gasping and flailing with her arms. She obviously couldn't swim.

I waded out and fished her back in to shore, more bedraggled than ever, and quite thoroughly waterlogged. She was still coughing and choking when I stopped her in the shallows and stripped her skirt from her. She was too dazed to protest.

I threw the skirt onto a rock, and nudged her until she sat down in the water. Then, with an occasional handful of sand and my left hand firmly anchored in her hair, I scrubbed her more thoroughly than she'd ever been scrubbed in her life. When I was finished, her skin was lighter and pinker, and she was a very docile little girl.

It was a pleasure to me just to amble along through the piney woods, breathing the scent of the resin that seemed to permeate the air, and not smelling either Rifka or myself at all. Rifka did not volunteer her opinion, but if she was silent and moody at least she was not openly sullen or angry. Adjustment to the continued presence of human being was still unfinished for me, and I did not object to her silence.

When darkness fell, we were still among the sighing trees, and I made immediate preparation to bed down. Rifka followed my example more slowly, and I noticed that she seemed to be watching me a little fearfully. a question, or questions, in her eyes. But she said nothing, and only curled up in her own nest of dry pine needles next to me.

I awoke, what must have been not so long after, to hear the sounds of soft sobs close by me.

I stared up into the night, past the overhanging, interlocked shadows of pine boughs, into the starry sky. Behind me the needles rustled, and the sobs choked into snuffles.

I turned over. Rifka was a pale and indistinct shape lying on the ground.

"What's the matter?" I asked. "Why're you crying?"

She snuffled some more, started to speak, choked, and began coughing. This brought fresh tears and her body shook with them.

Not knowing why I did it, I reached out and touched her hair. It was clean, dry, but tangled with bits of pine needles, and I combed it with my fingers.

It seemed to soothe her. She cuddled up against me, and her sobs quieted and her breathing slowed. Finally she said, "I hurt."

"You hurt? How?"

"My belly. All empty. No food. And . . . and cold. Night cold."

"Your belly . . .?" I repeated. "Food. When did you last eat?"

"Morning," she said, her nose still snuffly. "This morning."

"This morning?" I said, curiously. "Then why're you hungry so soon?" I hadn't eaten as recently myself.

She pushed herself up on her arms and stared into my face. Her lower lip seemed to tremble, and her face was streaked by the tears. My hand seemed useless in her hair; I let it fall to her bare shoulder. Unconsciously, I brushed away a couple of needles which had caught on her skin.

"You very strange man," she said. "You don't never eat? I eat two, maybe three times a day. Always before sleep, I eat."

It was a revelation to me. She'd missed a meal. I hadn't realized that. It would make quite a difference if I had to supply fresh food for the girl twice every day. Suddenly I felt my first qualms about bringing her with me.

"You not cold at night either?" she asked, poking at my skin with her finger.

It was cooler, of course. I'd noticed that. But it hadn't bothered me. Neither heat nor its absence seemed to hurt me. Sudden change might, but my body seemed to adjust quickly. The gradual cooling of night had no effect upon me.

But Rifka's skin, I discovered, had formed into a rash of tiny bumps, and I felt her body shaking. Her skin was very cool.

"Food I can't do anything about until tomorrow," I said. "But I can make you warmer."

I took off her skirt and my own. Opened flat, the two of them provided a cover which just stretched over us both. She pressed her body up along the length of mine, pulled the skins completely over her, and soon fell into the regular breathing of sleep.

I stayed awake for a long time, letting the questions flow freely through my mind, hoping for a few answers from those inner recesses of my mind which seemed to shelter so much knowledge. But none came. The heat of her body was comforting against my own, and the rhythm of her breath-

30

ing was a sound that lulled me, eventually, into my own deep sleep.

Food was the problem.

"Rifka," I said the next morning. "What do you normally eat?"

"Meat," she answered.

"How do you get the meat?"

"They hunt it. They kill it. The men, I mean." I was pleased to see she was beginning to speak more. Her vocabulary seemed to be expanding, as she picked up words, phrases, and usages from me. She learned quickly.

"Hmmm. That's no help. What sort of animals do they hunt?"

"Anything. Animals. Men. Anything with meat," she said. "You hunt for meat now?"

I shrugged. "I'm not much of a hunter."

She gave me a look which begged me.

" . . . But I'll try," I added.

And so I did. There seemed to be little but birds and the small furry things Rifka called "Squills" in the upper branches of the pines which covered the ridge, so I descended the ridge back to the west, towards the stream, which flowed down the same valley the ridge paralleled.

My reasoning was that animals like water, the larger animals needing water more often. The stream might attract something I could catch.

The pines thinned as the hillside grew rockier, and shrub brush became heavier, until at last I was skirting thickets to find my way downhill.

As I approached the stream, I heard a peculiar noise. Over the sounds of the stream itself, rushing and falling among stones in its bed, I heard a grunting and snuffling sound. It sounded half animal, half human, and I made my way carefully, in a low crouch. The rotten pine branch I'd picked up on the ridge above seemed a little silly gripped in my hand like a club, but I didn't drop it.

I clambered over an outcropping of rock that shelved out, and dropped into the brush again. Ahead, the noises were more distinct, but I could see nothing. I was afraid to chance standing up. I stopped, hunkered down on my heels, and listened.

The area was very quiet, except for the sounds which had drawn me. Perhaps it was a little *too* quiet. I heard no bird calls, none of the squills chattering at each other. It was as though the creature just beyond my screen of brush occupied the center of a large and empty stage.

It grew more quiet. The sounds had stopped. I caught my breath in my throat and held it. My pulse was loud in my ears. A breeze caught the leaves of the shrub over me and tickled them lightly against my back. A rustle like a sigh came and then was gone. I heard the thin buzzing of a tiny insect that paused for a moment to light on my arm. I wanted to move. My ankles ached from the strain, and my skin itched. I let my breath out, slowly, through my open mouth, a whisper only.

The brush before me crashed with a violence that rocked me back on my heels, and tumbled me off balance. I thrust an arm behind me to catch myself, and something huge and black reared up over me.

My first thought was, *It's too large!* It stood on its hind legs, like a man, its legs too stubby and short, its body too long, too tall. It held its forearms before it, paws raised, claws great stiff talons. Its fur gave off a warm, musty smell that was sudden in my nostrils. Its mouth gaped open, incongruously small, white and even, snout elongated and yet blunt, the nostrils in its black nose flaring. It stared into my eyes with a fierce pride and anger that told me I had violated its sanctuary and must die.

It towered over me, and seemed to regard me for a moment as I might have regarded an insect caught in my skirt. Then it grunted. It was a deep, *whoofing* sound.

I was trapped on all sides by the dense growth of low scrub brush. To my back the rock shelved upwards.

I came slowly to my feet, unfolding myself carefully.

The animal was still taller than I was, its body broader, heavier. I felt a shock from my right hand as I realized the club I still held was touching the rock behind me. I'd forgotten the club. It didn't seem a very effective weapon.

The beast opened its arms as though welcoming me home, at the same time making a low growl deep in its throat. Down its chest were two rows of nipples. A mother—with her young somewhere nearby. Protective: fierce.

I really wanted only escape. But that was impossible. I was hemmed in. The beast was so close I could smell her sour breath. Both of us seemed to be poised, waiting. For what?

I moved. I started to raise my arm.

And found myself suddenly, suffocatingly, locked in the creature's embrace.

I was smothered in thick, dusty, pungent fur, my face buried in it. Something warm and wet pressed against my chest. My arms were pinned at my sides, and her claws were raking my shoulder blades.

It was hard to breathe. My nose and mouth were jammed against her heavy fur, and she was tightening her hug around my chest. I knew, very clearly, that she was going to kill me.

I tried to struggle. My arms were already numb, and I had the feeling I'd dropped the club—not that it mattered. I couldn't move. I tried to throw myself into the sort of overdrive I'd used to overcome both the animal I'd eaten and Poll. Nothing. In this creature's grip I was powerless. I felt the bones of my ribcage grinding. I couldn't breathe at all. Claustrophobia swarmed over me in tiny optical flashes and sounds rung inside my head. My tongue was forced back into my throat as I tried—and failed—to draw a breath. A gagging sensation forced my mouth wide, and I wondered if this was the first spasm of death.

A ripple of tension went through me, and my nostrils were filled with the stench of burning fur. I felt myself going limp, as a black wave of exhaustion washed over me. I started to fall . . .

I jerked my eyes open as my knees crumpled under me. The creature—her death embrace—what had happened?

My eyes were tearing, and when I tried to raise my arm to wipe them dry, it refused at first. I let myself collapse until I was sitting, my back against the shelf that had blocked my retreat. Through blurry eyes I saw the crumpled heap of black fur that had been the she-beast. It was lying, unmoving, in the brush through which she had come. I stared at it without belief. It was not moving. It did not move at all.

Slowly strength came back to me. My hands trembled, my legs shook, but I could stand; I could move. My chest and back ached, but I could move. Nothing seemed broken. I looked at the dead beast.

She had fallen backward. The sun was high overhead, and the black fur of her belly had rusty tints in the bright light. A hole no bigger than my finger had been bored—burned—in her lower throat. It seemed to angle upwards. I found another hole, the same size, in the back of her head. It had killed her. It had singed her fur, seared her flesh, and cauterized her fatal wound. It was neat and precise. And it had killed her.

How?

I climbed the hill to the ridge. I found Rifka sitting under a tree, exactly where I'd left her.

"Come," I said. She looked at me, troubled perhaps by the rusty tone of my voice, but came quickly to her feet. I led her back down the hillside, through the brush, across the outcropping of rock, to the dead animal.

She looked at me with an expression of mixed awe and fright, pride and fear. "God," she said, using that term for the first time. "You killed a barr!"

The underbrush rustled at the sound of her voice. I jumped down to the ground next to the big creature.

There, nestled against the side of the female barr, shaking and whimpering, was a little barr.

CHAPTER FIVE

Rifka bent down over the little animal. It was not much bigger than a human baby. It was small and chubby, its head too big, with large rounded ears and wide unblinking eyes. It stared back at her as she murmured, "Poor baby, poor baby." Then it turned its head and began nuzzling again the unresponsive side of its dead mother. And again it whimpered. It seemed to know its mother was dead.

"A cub," Rifka said. Her tone was soft, as I'd never heard it before. "Poor thing. No mama now." She reached out her hands to it.

It made a snarling sound and drew back, pressing itself flat against its mother's side.

Rifka began crooning to it. "Poor baby, poor li'l barr cub. Ah, now . . ." She stroked its back, and then its head.

The cub's shaking subsided a little. It seemed reassured for the moment.

"Look," I said. "This is it; what're we going to do?"

"You killed its mother," Rifka said.

"You were hungry, remember?" I said. I didn't keep all the irritation out of my voice. "And it almost killed me, first."

She turned away from the cub then. "It almost kill you?"

"Yeah." I didn't like the memory.

"How you kill it?"

"I wish I knew," I muttered, more to myself than to her.

Rifka picked the cub up and placed it on its dead mother's chest, hoping it would suckle her breasts. But the cub took only a few, random licks at its mother's teats and then began whimpering once more.

Rifka picked the cub up again and cradled it in her arms, on its back. It blinked its eyes at her, sleepily.

"I take cub away. You make meat out of mama-barr," she told me, authoritatively.

"With what?" I asked.

She turned back. "No knife?" she asked. Then she shook

her own head in remonstrance. "You find something," she said.

It was wonderful to find someone with so much confidence in me.

It took me most of the afternoon, and five thin, slate-like pieces of stone to hack the fur off the barr and carve the meat into chunks. Periodically, I went to the stream and washed myself clean again.

The large skin I laid, fur down, on the flat rock shelf, and scraped until the sun was angling midway down to the west. Then I washed it, scoured it with sand, and washed it again in the stream. What I ended up with was a huge fresh fur hide.

The head I left behind. The meat I wrapped in large leaves which grew on a short tree nearby, and then, after lining the skin with more leaves, packed it inside the skin. The four legs could be tied together to secure it. When I swung it up onto my back, the load staggered me at first, but it wasn't impossible. I'd left well over half the total weight of the animal behind, as well as saving out a goodsized hunk of meat for Rifka's immediate meal. All in all, I was rather proud of myself. I'd certainly managed to secure enough food to take care of her for a while.

I found her sitting up the hill a ways, in a patch of grass in the open sun. She seemed to be gazing off into the distance, and the cub was nestled against her, its furry head between her breasts.

"It's hungry," she told me softly. "It tried to nurse me."

"Think it would eat meat?" I asked.

"Its own mother?" she said. Her tone was shocked.

"Why not? You have," I said. "And you *knew*."

That silenced her for a moment. Then, voice very small, she said, "It only takes milk. It too young."

"What're you going to do with it?" I asked. "Adopt it?"

"What *you* do?" she flared up at me. "You leave it here to die?"

"Is that worse than taking it with us to die?" I replied. "It's too young—you said that yourself. It can't live without its mother."

Our voices had awakened it. The cub opened its eyes,

36

and twitched its ears back and forth to catch the direction of our voices. It looked up at Rifka, then nuzzled its nose against her left breast. Its tongue curled out around her dusky nipple. But there was no milk. The cub made a little noise that sounded like a plaintive question, and looked up again at Rifka's face.

"You see? I no leave it. *Can't*."

I shrugged. I held aloft the hunk of meat I'd saved out. "You ready to eat now?"

She eyed the meat distrustfully. "You cook it."

I looked at her. I waited until her eyes returned to mine. Her stare was innocent.

"Cook it?" I said. "With what?"

She showed me with what. Granite rubble lined the stream. Pine needles and the dried twigs from the dead lower branches made fine tinder. It took a while. You struck and you struck and you struck. The sparks were tiny, and most of them too feeble to start any kind of fire. But some weren't, and you waited for them, waiting until one was struck, and then you nursed it, you nursed each one amid its dry nest of tinder, and you cursed as one after another died out with a tiny spiral of smoke, and you struck some more.

And finally one caught. And what was in one moment only a bright and dancing spark was in the next a hungry little flame, licking eagerly over the heap of tinder, and ready soon for bigger stuff—broken branches, also from low on the pine trees ("They always dry, always burn," Rifka told me; she obviously enjoyed finding a task in which she could instruct me), dried cones, fallen branches of greater girth (including my unneeded club)—until finally it was a roaring fire over a fine bed of coals.

I tore apart a green sapling to make a spit and its supports, and then we roasted the meat over the fire, its juices sizzling out to spark and spatter.

The smell overcame me. I'd thought I was no hungrier than the day before, or, indeed, the day before that, after eating. But something inside of me responded to the smell of roasting meat, and I found myself swallowing saliva frequently in anticipation.

At last she pronounced the meat done and ready. The

sun was a solid bar of orange beyond the next ridge west, and the fire glowed cheerily on the open hillside. Without knowing why, I felt nervous, eager to be done with the meal and move on.

We gnawed the meat from the common hunk, now shrunken, the spit, our handle, to be passed back and forth from hand to greasy hand. The flavor was strong, and the meat none too tender, but it satisfied the hunger I hadn't known I had. I wondered if I too would succumb to this habit of eating twice daily. Rifka laughed and chattered as we ate. The food had restored her spirits completely. Grease and black from the char smeared her face as she ate. And, after we'd both taken the edge from our appetites, she worried a small piece loose and gave it to the barr cub.

It sniffed at the meat and her fingers, but didn't seem to know what to do with it. Finally she had another idea. She popped the piece into her mouth and began chewing it vigorously. Then she took it out again and once more offered it to the cub.

"Mothers sometimes do that for babies," she said. She pushed the chewed piece into the cub's mouth with her finger. "Go on," she told it. "Eat."

The cub ate the single piece of meat, but try as she would, she could get it to eat no more. Soon the baby barr was once more snuggled asleep in her arms.

Twilight had fallen when we were finished eating. Rifka started to wipe her hands on her skirt, then found the cub occupying that part of her lap. "Wash," I said. I pointed down to the stream. "Use sand with water. Grease turns bad. Smells bad. I don't like it. Wash it off. Your face, too. Put the cub down. I'll watch it till you get back."

She didn't want to. She didn't want to give up the cub, and she wanted even less to go down to the stream and wash. But she took a couple of looks at me, and finally nodded. She handed the bundle of sleeping fur to me. "You take. Be good."

"Hey," I said. "Just a bit, here!" But I was holding the cub, and she was noisily stalking off down the hill. I sighed, and pulled the little thing closer, up against my lap and chest. It fidgeted in its sleep, but it didn't wake up. For some

38

reason, that gave me a warm feeling.

The light of the dying fire played against my eyes. The barr cub was a furry soft thing in my arms. The meal filled my belly. I was tired anyway. I'd spent an entire day, what with that barr and butchering and cooking it. It felt nice just to sit there and stare at the fire . . .

. . . waiting for Rifka . . .

My eyes flew open with a jerk. It couldn't have been too long. The fire was only embers. In the west, reflections of another dying fire. Overhead, the early evening stars.

Where was Rifka?

It didn't take that long to wash. Knowing Rifka's aversion to the idea, it shouldn't have taken half that long.

Carefully, I eased the sleeping cub down on the fur bundle that had once been its mother. It still slept.

I moved carefully and quietly back, away from the fire—uphill.

I slipped into the pines, where I could see the entire area around the fire. I saw nothing.

I moved along the hillside a ways, then began working my way down, through the brush, towards the stream.

What had happened to Rifka?

I kept an eye on the campsite when I could. No one seemed near it.

Near the bottom of the hill, I heard faint sounds. I moved toward them, carefully, slipping on all fours among the bushes. When I got closer I could tell they were muffled sobs of pain. I heard something else, too: the hoarse grunting of ragged breath.

Then I saw them.

He had her down, his body weighting hers, against the streambank. They were struggling, his hand clamped over her mouth. His body was bare, and he seemed to be pulling at her skirt. He had only one hand for the job, and she wasn't helping.

I don't think he ever heard me. She saw me, her eyes wide and staring directly at me as I stood over him. Perhaps her sudden limpness warned him—but not in time. Perhaps he was too stupid to recognize it for a warning. He was still pawing at her skirt when I caved the back of his skull in with the rock in my hand.

I don't think I intended to kill him. It wasn't what I'd planned. I wanted to stun him. That would have been enough. But maybe it wouldn't have been enough. I'd never tried stunning a man with a blow to the back of his head before. It was the heaviest rock I could easily handle with one hand. I didn't want to take chances. I was tired, worn out. Maybe I added too much muscle to gravity's work. But he was never real to me as a human being. I never even saw his face. Rifka said he was young. I never even saw that. I saw only the impossible dent in the back of his head and the wetness of blood. I didn't want to see his face after that. I'd had enough of killing for the day.

It was Rifka who made me wait while she pawed through his neat little pile of things. She explained it to me:

"I came to wash. I finish. I start back. He jumps me, this man. From out the bushes, his arm around my neck. I can't make noise."

"He saw our fire, on the hill," I said. "I knew it was dangerous, out in the open like that."

I washed my own hands and face.

"Look," she said. She held up two objects.

The first was a knife. It was obviously very old. The blade still shone, despite its nicks and scars. The handle was of rotten leather, wrapped in places with more recent additions, crude thongs. The blade was as long as my open hand from fingertip to wrist. I honed it against my palm to get the feel of it. The handle felt clumsy, but the knife was still well-balanced. I stuck it in the knotted thong of my skirt and took the second object.

This was another piece of metal, but where the knife was still bright, this piece was rusted, pitted, and very eaten away. It was an oblong, or once had been. It fitted in the palm of my hand. There were fresh scars on one side.

"Iron," Rifka said. "Steel-stuff, they call it. Fire-maker."

I struck it against a hunk of granite. The sparks were encouragingly thick: much thicker than before.

A hole ran its length, and another leather thong, much worn, was threaded through it and tied in a loop.

I slung the loop over the handle of the knife and let the fire-maker fall between the folds of my skirt.

Rifka carefully carried water up the hill in the skirt of

40

the dead man. We used it to wash down the fire, after the cub had had his nose dunked in it without showing any signs of wanting to drink. Then I once more shouldered the full bundle of meat, and followed Rifka, carrying the barr cub, up the hill. As I climbed, I wondered what sort of crazy family I'd burdened myself with.

Our morning meal the next day was prepared much more easily, since fire came quickly with the steel fire-maker. I found the knife a vast improvement in carving free a chunk of meat, and we were once more hiking northward before the sun was very high in the east.

Only one incident had marred our meal: the cub had again cried for food, and again swallowed only one tiny piece of pre-chewed meat. There was an innocence and trust in the baby animal that made our helplessness a knife of frustration that twisted in our guts.

At midday the itching along my back was too much for me, and I called a halt. When I let the fur pack fall, Rifka called out in surprise. "Your back! What happen?"

It was irritated; that I knew. The fur rubbed against it as my stride jogged it, and my sweat had soaked the fur and stung the irritation. But it was Rifka who discovered the half-healed gouges of the she-barr across my back.

Before they'd seemed scratches, and Rifka had hardly noticed. Now, the scabs worn loose and skin stretched and pulled, they were open sores.

"You let me look at you," she told me. "All over." And she began a minute examination of every scratch, bruise, or scabbed wound I had, from the scratches on my legs to the almost-healed bite in my left thumb.

There wasn't that much for concern. My ankles and wrists had the deepest wounds, but they were heavily crusted over and I felt only a dull ache from them now and then. Where my thumb had been bitten was fresh pink flesh, a little concave but unscarred. My arms and legs had tiny pink lines where scratches had been and healed.

"You mend fast," she told me.

"How long does it take you?" I asked.

She pointed to a scab on her knee. It was old-ish, worn away from kneeling. "I get that many days ago."

"How many?"

41

She tried to tell me. She held up first one, then two, then all her fingers. Her ability to count was limited. But she made her point. It hadn't happened yesterday. Nor the day before yesterday. And—such a small scab; she'd scraped herself kneeling on a rock—it was still not entirely healed.

She fussed over my back, inspecting and cleaning it, wiping it with some of the leaves I'd used to wrap the meat, using a piece of the meat itself as a poultice. I scabbed over quickly. She told me that a clear fluid oozed into the cuts, filling them and growing sticky, then frosting them over as it stiffened. It happened as she watched. She gave me a running account of it.

I wondered what she made of me. It was an impressive list she must have totaled by now. I could go long times without food, heat, and cold didn't hurt me, I was very strong, very fast, and—somehow—I'd mysteriously killed a barr without a weapon. I was virtually indestructible.

What did that make of me, I wondered.

Was I more, or less than human?

CHAPTER SIX

It was on our fourth day after I'd killed the cub's mother that Rifka said, "Tanner." She had taken to using my name more often, sometimes with a childish sort of delight.

This time her tone was not light.

"The baby-barr," she said, half crooning the name. "He's dying."

It was true: I'd seen it coming.

"It won't eat," she said, plaintively. "A bit I give it. But no more. Only that bit. I try meat raw. I try chewing meat, and a piece for baby-barr now and not-now."

"Now and then," I said, correcting her absently.

"Now and then," she said. "But it won't eat. Not much. Not enough. Now it's so weak. So sad." The barr cub looked from her face to mine. It was limp in her arms. It looked thinner. Its eyes seemed half-glazed, their focus vague. I looked back at Rifka's face. A trail of moisture was creeping down one cheek.

"What can I do?" she asked. "What can we *do?*"

"We can't save it," I told her. "If you had a baby, if you had milk, could nurse it . . . It needs milk. We have none."

"You killed its mother," she said, her tone accusing.

"I didn't know," I said, half-truthfully. I hadn't known about the cub, but I'd seen the mother had been nursing. "And I couldn't help it. It was trying to kill me."

"Yes," she sighed, not looking at me. "I know."

"I told you it would die," I said.

"I no care!" she cried, her tone reverting.

The cub made a whimpering noise. It sensed something was wrong with its adopted mother. It buried its head between her breasts, and one paw pulled feebly at the breast it lay against.

"What do you want to do?" I asked.

"What can I do?" she asked dully.

"Not very much. Two things: either keep on carrying the cub, caring for it, trying to feed it until it dies, or let it die now, quickly, and put an end to it."

"*No!*"

43

"You said it yourself. It's dying."

"Maybe, if I try more meat. Today. Maybe it learn ..."

I shrugged.

"It won't," she said, slowly agreeing. Then, "Nothing? I can't do nothing?"

I shook my head.

Tears flooded down her face as she looked up at me. "Here," she said. She held the cub out to me. "You take it."

I took the cub from her arms. It felt thinner, smaller, lighter. I fancied I felt its bones more sharply. Its fur was matted, no longer glossy. Some of the fur stayed on her arms and breasts.

"Take it away," she said. "Don't talk to me. Never tell me. Take it away and don't bring it back."

Then she fell over into a crouch, hugging herself and crying in loud sobs.

I walked away, and the sounds of her sorrow followed me. They followed far longer than they should, and I looked down at the little creature cardled in my arms and heard its own sad noises.

I walked across a carpet of pine needles and skirted up-thrust knobs of rock. I followed the aisles between the trees, trudging down the slopes and up the rims of hollows, backtracking on the way we'd come the day before, following a trail I hoped I'd never walk again.

At last I stopped by a pile of crumbled rocks below a weathered boulder. I sat down on the bed of pine needles, my back to the boulder, and stared off across the forest.

Shafts of thin golden sunlight slanted down through the trees, filtered and pale. A soft breeze touched my wet cheek. The pines sighed. A southern breeze, a warm breeze; comforting. But not very.

I laid the cub beside me, and it tried to cling to me, its mother's killer. It was too feeble, too weakened. It tried to raise its head and could not.

I drew my knife and did it quickly.

Then I piled rocks I could not see upon the body I would not look at.

And stumbled back.

The land changed. Pine forests became maple, oak, and

44

birch. The smooth brown carpet of needles became a mulch of fallen, rotting leaves, sometimes slippery over bare rock. Rock outcroppings were frequent, as were occasional scrub brush, and grassy clearings.

Game too was more common. Rifka pointed out the droppings of deer. The barr meat had grown too gamey to eat, and I threw what was left away when I killed my first deer. It was a perfect overhand throw with the knife, but it sank into the animal's tawny neck soundlessly—not at all the sort of heavy *thwock* with which it had embedded itself in practice tree trunks.

Frequently honed on smooth rocks, the knife was sharp and a fine tool. We cleaned the deerskin and added it to our traveling wardrobe. The barrskin was now our bed and blanket, and the deerskin became our new pack-larder. I carried it, Rifka the barrskin.

The elevation was climbing; the nights were cooler. The evening fire became more than a cooking fire. Rifka would pull the thick barrskin, fur against her skin, close around her shoulders, huddling before the fire while chewing her meat and licking her fingers. She slept now with her body intertwined with mine.

It was a curious life we spent in those weeks. We saw no other human being, saw and heard no sign of one. We traveled a countryside that had returned entirely to nature. Sometimes we saw the overgrown and fallen ruins that marked the sign of yesteryear's man. More often we did not. Little had survived. I wondered what had happened. Rifka did not know. She knew only formless superstitions about the Old Places——and no explanations at all.

In some ways those weeks were times of beauty and happiness. We had only one goal: to survive and push on. Some days we traveled long distances. On others—especially those infrequent days when the sky was overcast and rain fell intermittently—we traveled little if at all. Survival meant food and water. Food meant game, supplemented once in a while by the sweet wild berries we found.

My wounds mended quickly. There came a day when the itching stopped and the scabs fell away to leave my wrists and ankles unscarred and whole. My back took the longest to heal; the friction of the pack I carried was the cause of

45

that. But in time my back too was bare of marks.

We had no set distance to be traveled, and no road to follow. We walked, most often side by side, talking sometimes, silent more often. The sun was clean and warm on our bodies. My aim with the knife became more and more certain. We were well-functioning organic machines, taking our pleasures solely in this simple fact.

Only one thing dimmed my pleasure in the days that sped past. At first I had put Rifka's moodiness—times when she seemed closed and distant, her mind like her eyes focused elsewhere—to the necessary death of the barr cub. She had not spoken of it and we never spoke of it again, either of us. But I wondered at times if she did not hold me to blame, if she did not harbor a festering resentment of my role in the death of the helpless baby's mother and its own.

Yet, this seemed not to be the case. And after a time I concluded it was something else. Her moods seemed to come and go too quickly, anxious and irritable one moment, too full of laughter and excitement the next. Too often when we rose in the morning, the early dawn's dew still upon the ground, the air still brisk, she would give me deep, searching looks in which she seemed to me examining me for some quality which was not there. It was as if I was being measured, against some standard I did not—could not—know. She seemed to be waiting, as if for me to answer her unvoiced question, and then, as I might rekindle the cooking fire for breakfast, shrug and become distant, her questions yet unanswered.

We talked, but we did not speak of our thoughts, our inner feelings. I never told her from whence I'd come, never explained my unusual, un-human body powers. Those things lay outside our conversations. And so I did not ask her to give voice to the question with which she seemed to search me so often.

The hills tumbled into deeper valleys, and when we descended to the west again, we encountered our first human settlement.

It was on the banks of a broad river, not far from the site of extensive ruins. The stubbed footings of what had once been a bridge ran far out into the river, just downstream, and the contrast was vivid.

46

The settlement was of logs and scavenged materials from the ruins. It reminded me in a curious way of the great slab under which Poll and his family had lived. Here were people building, not with fresh materials, but with what they could salvage from among the old.

A wall of logs and rubble surrounded the settlement, enclosing perhaps a dozen dwellings. These were log-sided, flat-roofed, shacks. Men and women moved among them at domestic tasks. There were many young children running about, and among them furred animals Rifka called dawgs.

We were still high on the hillside, crouched behind concealing brush. "Dawgs!" she breathed, and she shuddered against me. "Dawg-men! They raiders. They come down to catch men. They send their dawgs after us. Dawgs run faster'n a man."

"This happened to you?"

"No, but I heard about it. And one time Mox, he bring dead dawg home. He *seen* them. They had, oh, *lots* dawgs. He threw a stone, killed a dawg, brought it home."

I stared down the hillside at the settlement. They looked little better than Poll's people. The shacks were arranged in no order, some built almost against others, sides angled in every direction. Yet, beyond the wall, I saw neatly tended rows of growing plants, gardens in which women stooped and worked. It was a peaceful enough scene. I wondered if to them the nomadic hunters to the south were little more than animals to be hunted down.

We did not approach the settlement any closer that day. Wary of my last contact with humans, I was content to wait until evening for what I wanted. We spread our barr fur out and settled ourselves on it and waited. Rifka made her deer-eyes at me again, then let her attention wander until she fell asleep in the westering sun. I watched the settlement.

Darkness fell. Hunters appeared, in twos and threes, packs of barking dawgs at their heels, stalking out of the lower forest. Most carried game slung over their shoulders and backs. Fires broke out like bright sparks in the settlement as evening meals were prepared.

Then, gradually, the fires died to tiny points that flickered and winked at me. Timbers had been pulled across the opening in the wall, effectively closing it off. The distant sounds of voices diminished, fading.

When the moon had risen and was well overhead, I touched Rifka lightly.

Her eyes flew open and she sprang into a sitting position. "Huh? What?"

"Time to wake up," I said.

She rubbed her arms briskly. "Cold. It's cold. I'm hungry, too. Why'd you let me sleep?"

"I thought you could use it," I said. "The day's not over yet——not for us."

"What you mean?"

"I'll show you. We're going down, now."

"Down there?"

I nodded.

"Why?"

"I'll show you," I repeated. "Let's go."

I'd mapped out our descent during the day, and the way was still clear in my mind. I led us down off the hillside without incident. Then we circled the settlement until we were just north of it.

The river lay silent and glossy to the west. Beyond it were the black silhouettes of distant hills and ridges. Close by, the wall of rubble made a jagged escarpment in the thin moonlight. And directly before us were the neat rows of plants.

I'd watched the women working in this garden during the daytime. I'd seen the plants they'd harvested, and their way of doing it. Here, by where we stood, there grew twisted, prickly vines, long green fruit hidden among their leaves. I searched until I found one, not much smaller than those the woman had picked, and I twisted it loose from its vine. Its skin was smooth and almost waxy, but little tufts of bristles grew in rows along its sides. "Look for more of these," I whispered.

"How many?"

"Just a few," I said. I'd taught her to count to ten—on her fingers—anyway. "We'll be taking other things, too."

"Why? What are these things?" she hissed back. "Ow! They hurt my fingers."

"Shhh," I cautioned.

We picked no more than half a dozen of the fruit. Next were thick balls of tightly wrapped leaves. I pulled two

48

from the ground, wondering what they contained inside them that could be eaten.

Stowing our plunder in my deerskin pack, we moved on. Next were hillocks with thin vines growing out from them. I pulled one from the ground at its root. Rifka uttered a gasp of surrpise when I pulled up a string of small tubers, the largest no bigger than half the size of my fist. As I'd seen the women do, I plucked them free and discarded the vine. We pulled up two more vines, but the third had only a single small tuber for us.

Next were long, pointed thick roots with a delicate lacery of above-ground plant. These had a pleasing pungent smell to them. I'd seen several small children wipe some clean of dirt and eat them raw, and the smell told me why.

Our pack was getting full. My last planned stop was a line of vines growing on a crude arbor. Round red fruit hung from these, black in the dim light, surrounded by smaller, green neighbors. The first one I picked squished in my hand; I hadn't expected it to be so soft. I licked my hand. It tasted good. On impulse, I bit a good chunk of the juicy fruit.

"You picked these to *eat?*" Rifka wanted to know.

"Sure," I said. "Try it." I held the remaining piece out to her.

She touched it with her tongue, then cautiously bit a small bite from it. She paused to taste it critically. "I dunno," she said. She reached out and took the rest and popped it into her mouth. "I . . . dunno . . ." she repeated, dubiously. I wanted to laugh. Instead, I began picking more of the fruit, careful not to poke my thumb into another one.

Rifka took the last one from me and stowed it in the pack on my back. "All full," she said.

"*Arrr . . . wow!*"

It came from the wall almost directly above us. Rifka let out a squeak. "*Dawg!*" she said. She didn't whisper.

Pandemonium broke out. The air filled with yelps, whines, barks, and growls, the sound of every dawg in that settlement——a sound that would wake every man, woman, and child within miles.

"Oh, God," Rifka said. She didn't have to whisper any

more. In fact, I couldn't have heard a whisper.

I drew my knife. Human shouts were added to the barking dawgs. The sounds were growing louder.

I looked back across the way we'd come.

The moon was bright and high overhead now. The open grass cast no shadows. If we ran back across that empty land, we'd be seen, and quickly followed. And besides, what had Rifka said? *The dawgs could run faster than a man.*

The shouting was closer now. Soon they'd be peering over the wall at us.

"Run," I said. I pushed her into a broken lope.

"But—this way—river," she panted back over her shoulder at me.

It was the only way I could think of. The dawgs could maybe *run* faster than men . . . but in the water?

There was just one other thing I'd seen from my vantage-point on the hill——and I led Rifka straight for it.

Behind us, the shouts became angry screams, and I knew we'd been seen. A stone thumped into the grass at—almost under—my feet. I kept running.

"Tanner!" Rifka screamed, tripping and falling. I stopped and wheeled. Pale shapes were jumping from the wall, into the garden. Four-legged ones followed, yelping. Another stone sailed out of the darkness. I ducked it.

"My foot! It hurts!" She'd turned her ankle.

I yanked her up with my free hand, gripping her wrist. "Doesn't matter," I shouted. "Run, damn you! Run or be killed!"

She ran.

And there, at the water's edge, pulled up on the bank, were the boats. They were crudely made of split timbers, with square, blunt ends. There were five. Clumsy paddles lay in each one.

"Help me!" I grunted, throwing my pack in the nearest and running to the next to bend and heave my shoulder under it.

We shoved all four off into the water, where they began drifting lazily. Then the fifth, with our pack. I pushed Rifka over the end and into it. "Sit," I told her, then, as the boat tipped dangerously under her shifting weight, "Don't stand up! Sit!" I waded further out, pushing as best I could against the slugglish water that was now at my chest.

I heard a splashing behind me, and turned, one hand on the edge of the boat.

A dawg, light grey in the moonlight, threw himself at me.

I thrust out my knife and caught him under his throat, ripping upward through his neck. Blood from his jugular sprayed me in great spurts, as he gave one last high-pitched yelp. Then he fall back into the water.

The ground dropped out from under my toes, and I stumbled, almost losing my grip on both the knife and the boat. Then I felt Rifka's hands on my wrist, pulling at me, and I let myself float up to the surface, and pulled myself over the boat's edge and into it.

As we paddled out onto the broad and slow-moving surface of the river, the outraged howls of the villagers behind us rent the night. We heard a lot of splashing, but nothing else. Once we were well out in midstream I paused to dip one of the pointy roots into the water to wash it. Then I bit off a chunk and began chewing it while I paddled again. Behind me, I heard Rifka chewing on another.

PART TWO

CHAPTER SEVEN

"You were lucky, of course," Rudo assured us.

I licked the meat juices from my hand. "I'd wanted to cross the river anyway," I said. "It was wide for swimming." (Rudo grunted a quick laugh at that.) "I'd seen the boats. They weren't far from the garden. I'd thought of them."

Rifka sat quietly beside me. Her belly was full. She sipped from the water jug and remained silent as our host repeated, "But you *were* lucky. They are a fierce people, the Kipsis. They've invaded our land from time to time."

"If we'd been lucky, the dawg wouldn't have barked," I said.

Rudo laughed. His laughter was full, deep from the gut. It shook his thick grey hair, his beard, and the stomach he hid behind his clothes. "I like you, Tanner," he said. "You're the first savage I've met I could talk to, you know that?"

I glanced across the rug, to the wall behind him. Driven into the logs of the wall were pegs, and hanging from the pegs were dark hanks of once-human hair. The skin of a striped animal took up the rest of the wall. It glowed dully orange in the fire light.

"That's just as well, isn't it?" I said. "But I'm not a true savage—not the kind you mean."

"No? You admit you come from across the river and to the south," Rudo said, his heavy brows knitting together. "You wear only a crude loinskin. You have only a scavenged knife, an old axe-head for striking with flint, a bearskin, a deerskin, and a bare-breasted woman." (Rifka's hand closed tightly over mine.) "Why, it's lucky they didn't just shoot you down when they saw you across the fields."

"They didn't."

52

"They couldn't believe what they saw. Milko is getting senile. He hasn't seen a good raid on this village in thirty years. If the entire people of the Kipsi rose from the grasses at the wall, he'd drop into his grave. He had to wait until he could see you standing before him. And that was a good bit too late."

Yes; by then I had put my knife to his ancient ribs, told him we were friendly, and suggested we go inside.

It was simple, really. My job was to go among the humans, talk to them, see them, get to know them. I wasn't going to be able to go on skulking about them forever, stealing from their garden patches in the night and running away from them afterwards. I had to approach them, win the confidence of at least a few. There was another kind of hunger in me: a desire to meet and talk with men.

So I had put it to old Milko, keeper of the gate: "I don't want to hurt you, and I don't want you to hurt me. Right? I'm a traveler, and I've come a long way. May I come inside?"

The old man had squinted at me from watery eyes. "Put that knife away," he said in a still-strong voice.

"Okay," I agreed, slipping it into my leather skirt.

He looked me up and down, then stared at Rifka, who tried to be brave, and stared resolutely back.

"Just you two?"

I nodded.

"Okay," he said, his tone not quite believing the words he uttered. "Come with me. You can meet Rudo." He nodded at the two spearmen atop the wall, and they relaxed their stance. That relieved me a bit.

Rudo was a man-mountain. He was big all over. He was clearly cut out for his role as bearded patriarch for the village. More important, he was friendly. He took in the sight of me with no great pleasure, but after we'd exchanged a few sentences he grew warmer, and bade me sit with him for the dinner meal (I'd timed our approach well). He had it served us in his dwelling from the cookfire outside. And there, between bites of meat, cooked tubers, and raw green leaves (I recognized them as being from the interior of the same kind of thick round leafy plants as we'd taken) on which other cooked vegetables were served, he questioned us affably.

"But you're not a savage, you say?" he persisted.

I smiled. "Do I talk like one?"

"No. That's what confuses me. You look like one, you smell like one, but you don't act like one. Why not? Where do you come from, Tanner?"

I sensed Rifka's own interest in that question. Where *did* I come from? She twisted around to look up at my face.

I wondered what I could tell them that would satisfy them, make sense for them, without telling them the truth. I shied away from the explicit truth; I didn't know why.

"I come from the south," I said. "We were an exploring party, on a boat, on the water. A storm hit us, and I was washed ashore. No one else survived. I lost all my clothes, my possessions."

"Ah! Then *she*" (a nod at Rifka) "wasn't with you?"

Had that been a mistake? No.

"Not then. I found myself in a vast city of ruins. There was only water to the south, east, and west. I came north."

"*The City,*" Rudo breathed. "You were in the City . . ."

"It's dead, buried under foliage," I said.

"The last of the Old Places," Rudo said. Rifka's hand tightened again on mine. "Yes, I can see your wanting to leave it. But the girl? How———?"

"I found her among the savages," I said, abridging it a little. "She wanted to escape. They'd captured her. I took her with me."

Rudo smirked. "I can see why."

I couldn't. Not, at least, in the way he seemed to think. I passed over it. "We've had only what little I took from a savage, and the skins of animals I killed myself. It hasn't been a lot, but we've done well."

Rudo's expression changed. "The bearskin—you killed the bear yourself?"

"I was lucky," I said.

A slow smile spread across his face, and then Rudo laughed, his laughter booming out into the night. "Lucky!" he choked. "Yes! Yes, you are!"

We were bedded down amid a heap of furs in a corner of Rudo's house. I felt uncomfortable, vaguely claustrophobic. The single-roomed dwelling was full of stale air and unfamiliar odors. I felt closed-in, entrapped. I wanted the fresh tang of the outside night air. Rifka's soft body was no comfort now; the heat of her only added to my discomfort. I did not sleep well.

But I dreamed . . .

I dreamed of the machine in which I'd first found myself . . . but a machine subtly different. I was running through its narrow corridors and metallic passageways, the air sterile and smelling faintly of machine oil. I had to get somewhere, be somewhere; I didn't know where.

You must hurry——they're cutting my circuits, said the Com-Comp; its voice rang inside my head, and my body seemed to speed up, moving faster and faster, leaping down the corridors in great bounds.

But I never seemed to get anywhere. Always, around each turning, beyond each portal, there were more of the metal mazes, spiralling in and around itself until if I was running down the same passageways again I could not have known it, so lost was my sense of direction.

Then, the entire scene dissolved, and I was standing on a great grassy plain that stretched to the horizon in every direction. Overhead the sun was a brassy blare, and kneeling before me was . . . *her* . . .

Her hair was the red of leaping flames, her skin pale and unblemished. Her body was perfectly formed: an open invitation. I knew her. She was the girl I had dreamed of before. The sight of her made me ache, and I reached down my hand for her.

Her face seemed to alter. Her hair grew wild and knotted, her body smaller, skinnier. She looked up at me from the mask of Rifka's face.

Suddenly a bolt of lightning struck down from the sky, smashing the ground around us. I looked up to see the sky boiling with dark clouds, shafts of violent light flashing back and forth among them.

Once again lightning struck. The heat of it singed me, and I leapt back. My face was seared. Where *she* had been there was nothing. Nothing at all.

I wanted to weep, and I had no tears. My face was a mask. I took it off, and looked at it.

I stared into my own eyes, and an electric shock hit me.

"Tanner!"

I felt her calloused fingers on my shoulder. Her breast was pressed flat against my shoulder blade. It felt sweaty. I opened my eyes and at first saw only darkness.

"Tanner—you okay?"

I felt dizzy, disoriented. My mouth was very dry, my nostrils hot and dry. I felt a strong thirst, and a desire for cool, sweet air. "No," I mumbled. Then, "Just dreaming."

"You cried out," she said. Her mouth was close to my ear, and I could feel her hot breath. It made me nervous. I tried to pull away from her.

"Tanner?"

"What?" I was irritated.

"You don't . . . like me?"

"Rifka, go back to sleep," I said, climbing off the furs and standing up.

"What's the matter?"

"Nothing. I'm hot. I don't feel good. I'm going out for some air."

"Oh," she said, and fell back on the furs. She rolled over, her back to me.

I picked my way past the sleeping bodies of Rudo and his fat wife, and went outside. I felt lousy. I wondered why.

"My son, Gonn," Rudo said, introducing us to a husky young man clad in leathers. Gonn had his father's broad face, but his beard was thinner and black, and there were fewer lines around his mouth and eyes. He was tall, big-barreled, a man like his father in many ways of appearance and mannerism. He studied us both, his eyes returning several times to Rifka's half-unclothed figure. "Gonn is a fine hunter," Rudo added with fatherly pride.

Rudo had been showing us around the small settlement where a little over one hundred lived. Gonn had a large buck deer strung up on a frame and was butchering it. His hands were bloodstained, and he wore a leather apron over his other clothes.

Gonn nodded. "I have a good throwing hand," he said.

"Tanner—he can throw the knife better than I ever seen," said Rifka suddenly.

Gonn's eyes narrowed a little, then he smiled affably. "So," he said. "A contest, perhaps?"

56

I hesitated. This man had grown up with hunting weapons. I had no great confidence in my own prowess, compared to his.

"Come on," he said, prodding me with a bloody finger. The buck's head lolled down from the frame, its large eyes fixed expressively upon me. I wondered if Rifka's boast had stung the young man.

I nodded. "I haven't had a lot of practice," I said.

Gonn led the way to the log wall. He had a piece of fresh deerskin in his hand. With a handy stone, he drove a peg through it and into the soft wood of the log. The deerskin was no larger than my hand. It was a patch of brown against the dark and peeling bark of the logs. We paced back thirty paces from the wall. Gonn took off his apron. Rifka stayed close behind me, while Rudo looked on, beaming. By ones and twos others drifted over. A small naked boy ran up and grabbed Gonn's legs. Gonn reached down and tousled his hair, then gave him a spank that sent him flying off again.

"The deerskin, or closest, best times out of five," Gonn said. He was telling me; not asking.

"All right," I agreed. "You first."

His knife was the same he'd been using to skin the buck. Like mine, it was clean of rust and shiny. Gonn plunged it into the dirt several times to cleanse it of blood. Then he whipped his arm back, went back on one foot, the other outthrust before him, and his arm blurred.

Thonk!

The blade struck just to the left and low, outside the skin.

I eyed the target, letting my eyes bring it into sharp focus. I kept my eyes on it. I let my fingers fit themselves loosely, comfortably, around the knife blade, along its back. I drew back my arm. The deerskin was tiny in the distance, but it filled my entire field of vision. I let my body move.

I didn't feel the throw. I wasn't aware of the moment when the knife left my hand. It was one clean movement, and it ended in——

Thonk!

——the center of the deerskin.

The crowd was silent. Gonn had laughed easily when

he'd made his throw. Now he did not laugh. I looked around. Over a dozen stood behind us.

"Four more," Gonn said, and I followed him to the target.

My own knife was imbedded an inch or more in the wood behind the deerskin. Gonn's was half buried. He worked it up and down twice, then his shoulder muscles seemed to bunch for a moment, and it was free. I yanked mine loose and we walked solemnly back to the others.

I wondered why we were doing this. It seemed childish. The hours I had spent throwing my knife before had been well-spent, since they had honed this new skill into sharpness for me. But competing, before others, to see who was the best throw with a knife——why? One of us must lose. But who would win? And for what reason?

Gonn's second throw was into the deerskin. A soft sigh passed like an expanding ripple among our audience.

My second throw hit the deerskin dead center, not a finger's width from where I'd stuck it before. Rudo chuckled, nervously.

Gonn's third throw was wild—high and to the right, the second log over from the deerskin. I put mine in the same area in which I had before.

His fourth throw was directly on target: the same spot I'd hit before. I heard him release his breath as if he'd been holding it until now, and caught, from the corner of my eye, the mocking look he aimed at me.

Sparks flew in the bright sun. My knife slashed the thongs wrapped around his handle, stuck the guard, spun in the air, and dropped to the ground.

"How shall we count that?" Rudo asked of no one in particular.

"It fell to the ground," Gonn said. "The round is mine."

"No," cried Rifka. "He hit your knife. If your knife not there, his'd be there!"

There was a murmur of agreement in the crowd.

"The deerskin, or closest," Goon quoted himself. "He didn't hit the skin. His knife is in the ground."

"If it was deer, he'd'a brought it down," Rifka flared angrily.

"Let it go," I said. "Once more, right?"

Gonn nodded. "Once more."

I had him flustered, I knew. Four times my knife had flown for the same small spot. Only the coincidence of his knife being there had deflected my last throw. I'd easily demonstrated my ability to throw accurately, and the fifth round was meaningless. We both knew it. Everyone watching knew it. Only Gonn could hope to best me on the final throw. Only Gonn felt the sting of pride, and had to try again, hoping for some miracle.

Once more he went through his elaborate throwing stance and loosed his blade. I wondered how many deer would hold still for such nonsense. His knife knicked the top of the deerskin. It, at least, would wait obligingly.

I raised my own knife and once more drew back my arm. I focused on the target, letting it grow in my eyes until it filled my vision. I stared at the cluster of cuts that scarred its center, and felt the easy weight of the knife in my hand.

——And flung it high and wild as something bowled into my legs, upsetting my balance and knocking my eyes off-target.

I looked down to see the dirty face and tanned body of the little boy. He had one arm around my knees, and was trying to climb me like a tree.

"I win, hey?" Gonn said, flashing a smile.

"*You?*" Rifka said, her tone shrill.

"Three outa five," he said. "Best of five, like I said."

"You won only the last two," I said, keeping my voice even.

"Huh!" he said. "You dumb savage. You can't even count."

"I count," Rifka said, loudly. "I count to ten." She held up both hands, fingers wide. "I count good. Tanner, he win first three times." She displayed three fingers on her right hand. "Gonn, you win two times." She held up two fingers on her left hand. "That's all!" She stuck out her tongue at him.

"*Rudo! Rudo!*" shouted a man running out from between two houses. The side of his face was a dark mass of blood. "*Kipsis!* Kipsis attack!"

Then he tripped, and fell flat on his face.

He didn't get up.

CHAPTER EIGHT

I found myself running with the others across the village. Screams and shouts filled the air, and everywhere men and women and children were running. I felt a hand catch at my arm, took a look back over my shoulder, and saw it was Rifka, following. Her hand slid down my arm and into my hand. We kept running.

Suddenly Rudo was standing before us, his body a huge bulk between the walls of two huts, blocking our way.

"You! Tanner! Is this your doing?"

It was, I realized later. The Kipsis had taken my raid on their garden for something more than it had been. They'd tracked me down to this village. Now they were retaliating. It would be the first war between the two villages in many years.

But all this came to me later.

"No," I shouted. "I know nothing of it. I run to join your battle."

He shook his head. "Can you use the bow?"

"No." Not yet.

"You would be no help to us."

"He can throw the knife," Rifka blazed angrily. "Your Gonn, he cheats, but my Tanner very good with the knife!"

Rudo smiled for a moment, the sun breaking through the winter of his face. "Once thrown, his knife is gone, child," he replied. "We do not throw knives now; we fire arrows, throw spears."

"Look," I said. "We're your guests here. We will help, any way you say, but let's not just stand here, mouths flapping in the wind!"

"Hokay," Rudo said. He turned. "Come!"

We followed his easy lope across the open center of the village, between huts, toward the far wall and the sounds of fierce battle.

Men were boiling furiously around the wall. Some were mounted high on it while others toiled below. Rocks fell among them, and sometimes bodies, and yet no one paused. Only the women, sobbing or wailing, would drag free the sometimes writhing bodies to minister to them.

As near as I could tell, the first line of defense was the men on the wall. I had no way of seeing what the Kipsis were doing outside the wall, but these men were firing arrows and spears and sometimes hurling rocks with a steady outpouring upon the attackers. Below, other men brought sheaves of arrows and spears, passing them up to the others above in a continuing stream. And, every so often, a man would leap up upon the wall to replace a fallen comrade.

I joined the throng hustling weapons at the base of the wall, standing in place between two bearded sweating men, taking what was given me and passing it on, up the wall. Rifka disappeared, and when next I glimpsed her, she was leaning over the bloody figure of a man who had fallen just beyond me, his head torn open by a heavy stone.

Everywhere around me, men shouted, screamed, and bellowed with anger and enthusiasm. And from beyond the wall I could sometimes hear the answering calls and shouts. The sound of their own cries seemed to bolster both sides' morale.

It didn't seem so much like a war, but more like some deadly earnest game, until the man we were passing to tumbled down among us, the thick shaft of a spear lodged in his chest. Blood frothed his lips and as he gasped for life red bubbles foamed in his mouth. He choked and, in the brief moment after he'd fallen, he died.

The man I'd been passing to looked confused. He was holding four spears bundled in his arms, and there was no one to pass them up to. The rhythm was broken. He looked around wildly, the whites of his eyes large and rolling.

"Up there, you Bolx!" shouted the man next to me.

But the man was frozen. He stank with fear. He did not move.

I scrambled past him and made the top of the broad wall in a running jump. Gratefully, it seemed, Bolx resumed his chore, passing the four spears up to me.

I paused to look out upon the battle.

The field was trampled and matted, bodies dotting it. But there were no nearby attackers at whom I might throw my spears. Instead, I saw men running away, away from the village, across the field and already nearly into the trees.

"What's this?" I called to the man at my right.

"They run," he answered. "Suddenly they turn and run." He gave a gleeful shout that was quickly picked up by others on the wall. "They run, they run!"

It made no sense to me. I watched them as they disappeared into the cover of the trees.

Nearby, a man lying on the grass gave a heave, turned over onto his back, and let escape his death cry, a ghastly wail of pain and rage. His chest was an open wound.

Off a little way I saw a man crawling for the trees. He was on his hands and knees, and moaning and whimpering. He was too far from the trees. He wouldn't make it. He seemed to realize it, and he rose upright on his knees to cry out in anguish to his comrades.

Their answer was the ominous curl of smoke from a place near the edge of the trees.

I pulled at the arm of the man dancing and shouting so gleefully next to me. "Hey," I said. "Look!" I pointed.

Now smoke was twisting up from other places along the edge of the open grassy field. The grass was brown and dry, and hungry to be consumed. The smoke spread, and pale flames leapt into sight.

My companion stared at this with his mouth agape, unbelievingly. Then he let out a bloodcurdling scream that tore at my ears. "*Fire!*" he screamed, pointing. "*Fire, fire!*"

It was quite a production, but among the general bedlam it took time to penetrate. Then, suddenly, more men were pushing up on the wall, crowding in around me and the others.

The flames were an advancing wall, now, spanning hundreds of yards in length. The breeze was behind them, urging them on.

The man in the field was still on his knees, still crying out to his fellows. Someone beside me elbowed me as he fitted an arrow to his bow and loosed it. The shaft embedded itself in the crying man's back, driving him forward into the grass and silencing him. Soon the fire was racing through his hair.

The man beside me gave a grunt of satisfaction, for what

reason I could not guess. I turned and looked at him. It was Gonn. I found my way back down off the wall.

The fire did no real damage to the wall. The grass burned too quickly. The flames rushed up to the wall, licked for a few moments at the heavy logs, sent a few fingers up loose shreds of bark, then died. Arms of fire swept around the village on each side, but failed to even scorch the gardens, the bare cultivated ground stopped them cold. The end result was a blackened field that would provide no more cover that season, the partial cremation of the fallen Kipsis, and a stalemate. The Kipsis did not return to attack again. Perhaps they felt avenged.

That evening, as we shared food with him again in his home, Rudo was solemn and pensive. He seemed several times on the verge of saying something, always to lapse again into silence. I sensed that his mood reflected that of the village. Since the abortive raid, we had been kept away from the villagers and avoided by them when possible. It added up to something, and I wondered when it would break.

"Umph . . . Tanner . . ." Rudo belched and wiped his hands. Okay, maybe this was it.

I looked up expectantly.

"Ahh, this is not an easy thing to say."

I waited.

"Well, I——oh, hell! Tanner, you've got to go." The words began spilling out of him, the dam of silence cracked and crumbling. "You're a savage to my people, you and your woman. That's one thing. They're not a bold lot, taken in all, Tanner. They're always a little afraid of the unknown, of the different. You—well, you're different. That's one thing.

"Another thing is that raid. See, the Kipsis, they live a good ten miles away and across the river. Not so close, but not that far away either. Maybe we're not the best of friends, but we get along. They stay on their side, we on ours. No trouble. Not for a long time.

"So, okay, we sat here, right here in my house, and we laughed about them, and their dogs and their boats. A funny story, yes? And that was last night. Today they attacked. *Why* did they attack? You know, my friend, as I

63

know. And I tell no one else, but my people——they know. They know it is *something* to do with you. Yes? Right? A savage, a pair of savages show up at the gates one day, and the next the Kipsis, people they don't know for many years, are attacking. Like an arrow nocks into the string of a bow, it fits.

"Also——" He held up his hand. "Also there is my son. I am not proud of my son today, Tanner. Gonn became less than himself. He became boastful, deceitful, a bad-tempered child. I do not like him thus. It belittles a man whose son is belittled. And it saddens me to say that Gonn has not yet stopped. Even now he may be stirring up my people against you. You did this to him—you showed him up and made him less a man. He cannot forget it of you. Nor can I. It comes between us now, Tanner, this thing. You are a man after my own heart, but less so now, and because of this.

"And yet, and yet . . . I want no more trouble. We lost men today, but no deed will bring them back to life, and I will have no more blood shed here. I want no trouble, but yet I see it coming.

"You must go. Take your woman with you, and leave. Tonight. Soon, when the others are sleeping." He stopped, run down, finally empty of words.

I nodded. "I'm sorry we brought this grief upon you, Rudo. We'll go." Rifka clutched at my hand, but said nothing.

Rudo looked relieved. "That's good. But I have a good surprise for you. You will not leave as poor as you came. Wait a moment." He rose, his figure suddenly bulking in the dim light, and strode to the door. He spoke there to someone outside, then turned and came back to his place across from us. And behind him came another.

The man was tall, dark, and thin in the uncertain light. I could not make out his features, or guess his age. His full beard was black and concealed his lower face. He moved easily, with a fluid grace. He seated himself.

"This is Avram. He is, I think, a man like yourself, Tanner. At heart he is a wanderer. He is our far-ranger, and each season he speaks of wandering beyond return. So far, he has not. *Yet,* eh, Avram?" He knuckled the man in the ribs with a laugh. "He lusts to see the lands beyond the hills, our Avram." Light from the embers of the cooking fire caught glints in the man's eyes. They were alert, alive. He had said nothing yet, but already I had some feel of the man.

"To take the sting off, Tanner," Rudo said. "I'm sending Avram with you. Two wanderers, eh?"

The lean man bent forward. "Which way do you go?" His voice was low, controlled. It was as I thought: a man of precision, few waste movements, few waste thoughts.

"Which way would *you* go?" I parried.

He smiled. "It would depend. There are four directions. To the east, the sun rises, but from out of the great water. There is little land to the east. The south . . . perhaps you know of the south. I am told you come from the south. But immediately south are the swamps and the joining of the rivers and the Old City. To the north, I cannot say, but the land grows colder in that direction, and already the summer is old. Westward, now . . . there the sun sets, and who can say where it is she sets?" His face softened. "Often I have stared at the setting sun and I have asked myself that. For me, that is where I would go."

I nodded. "To the west, then. . . . That suits me."

"Good!" Rudo said. "Let us set about outfitting you, then."

The moon was full in the sky, its light bright on the sleeping village, when Rudo closed the gates behind us. The field beyond the walls was black, the charred stubble brittle and crumbling under our feet, the dust of ashes pungent with the smell of death. We followed the wall of the village around half its perimeter, and then struck off to the west for the dark shadows of the forest.

We were well provisioned. I'd been dressed in leather leggings and a belted tunic that fitted not too badly. Rifka wore a cloak that fell around her like a tent, obscuring all but her calves and feet. Avram, of course, wore the clothes with which he'd first joined us: an outfit not unlike mine. He had low moccasins for his feet, and moved upon them as though he wore nothing at all. We both bore packs, and Rifka the bearskin, a prize with which she would not part. It hung over her shoulders, an outer skin over her cloak. My knife was in my belt, and my iron fire-maker. Avram had bow and arrows slung across his back, outside his pack. We'd been given smoked and salted meats and root vegetables, and both Avram and I had water-skins at our belts, animal bladders filled fat with the water of a nearby spring.

Once under the trees, we followed a narrow trail that showed signs of frequent use by men. It was, Avram said, a trail commonly followed a way by hunters. It would lead, he said, to one of the Old Ways, a great road that left scars on the mountains. "I have gone that far—no farther. But the road leads west."

The trail twisted and turned, dipping into gullies and climbing steeply along hillsides. Roots stretched their gnarled and ropy fingers across our way, and rocks thrust up at unexpected places. The moon cut through the whispering leaves of the trees overhead in jagged patterns, and the shadows were deep and deceptive. It was hard going for us all.

Finally, Rifka stopped. "Tanner. I—I'm too tired." I looked up through the trees and tried to estimate the position of the moon. It hung high in the west. Two hours—three? It had been a long day.

"We'll stop now," I said. "Bed down." I looked around.

Avram pointed ahead. "A glade, not far."

"Okay. A little farther, Rifka?"

She shrugged. We trudged on.

Once, during the night, I felt Rifka's arms go around my chest, clutching me. I was stirred from my sleep. *A bad dream?* I wondered. She squirmed against me. Her body was hot, her skin slippery with sweat as it pressed against mine. But then I fell back into deeper slumber, and I remember no more. And in the morning, she said nothing.

We awoke late. The sun was already above the treetops to the east. I was pulling on my leggings when Avram unrolled himself from his bedding and sat up, knuckling his eyes. He glanced over at me and made a grimace. "Late," he said. He stretched his arms outward. "Overslept." His eyes moved away from me and to Rifka, climbing into her brief skirt. For a moment his face was empty of expression. Then he climbed to his feet. "Best we eat quickly, move on."

66

"Any chance we'll meet others along this trail?" I asked.

He shook his head. "No. Not yet. Too early for our hunters."

"What about other villages?"

"None to the west."

"None?"

"None we know of." He shrugged. "If we go far enough . . . who knows?"

Rifka had a fire burning, and we ate in silence. It was my first chance to size up Avram in broad daylight. What I saw did not contradict my impressions of the night before. A thin face, heavy dark brows over narrow, close-set eyes that seemed set deep behind a permanent squint. A sharp nose that jutted out over a thick mustache and beard, lips a thin line half hidden, stolidly set. His skin was a burnished tan, his hair receding from a lined forehead. I revised my estimate of his age upwards by ten years. And I wondered how long he had dreamed of this trek, of breaking free of his home, his village, and his life as he'd known it. A curious blend of the dreamer and the practical man.

"Like an animal." Rifka whispered to me as Avram moved off briefly into the bushes. "He moves fast, quiet, like an animal."

"What do you think of him?" I asked.

She gave me an oblique look that told me nothing. "He does not boast," was all she'd say.

CHAPTER NINE

With considerable meandering, the trail eventually led us to the Old Way. It was a great swath of crumbling concrete, overgrown in places by grass and bushes. *And it jarred me.*

We had climbed a low hill, and then we were overlooking the ancient roadway. It twisted out of sight to the southeast, cut directly across our path, and then angled through great cuts in the hills to the northwest.

I'd seen that stretch of road before.

. . . Once the concrete had been white and new, dual strips divided into four lanes, along which wheeled vehicles raced at great speeds . . . I seemed to have a vivid picture in my mind that fitted over the reality before me, superimposing itself over my vision . . . I saw flat, wedged-shaped machines of bright colors pursuing one another around curves——across which dirt had washed and grass had grown . . .

"Tanner?"

Her voice broke the spell, and once more I saw only old scars and ways long disused. *But I had been here before.* And I knew for a certainty that it had been in the days when the roadway was young and new.

I did not feel the warmth of the sun, nor feel the stirrings of a breeze. I heard not the call of nearby birds, nor the close buzzings of gnats.

"Something wrong?" Avram asked.

I shook my head. "Nothing. Let's go."

We descended the hill, crossed a gully, and climbed the grading to the roadway itself. I kicked at a section of concrete, and it broke apart into rotten pebbles and dust.

"Tanner—this thing, what it it?" Rifka asked.

"A road," I said. "One of the old roads."

"But look: ahead, it cuts the hill in two!"

"It is said," Avram offered in a rare burst of loquaciousness, "that the Ancients forced open the skies and made lightning to strike, to carve them this roadway." He was addressing himself more to Rifka than to me.

I smiled. "More likely they simply built it themselves, as they did their cities."

Avram did not reply.

We followed the road to the north and northwest. We saw no signs of others before us. In places, hillsides had fallen or washed across the drainage ditches and cut across the roadways, sometimes with no more than a thin layer of soil, other times blocking the way and forcing us to detour. On one such occasion, an arm of a towering hill stretched out across the road to the foot of an opposite hill, and tall oaks grew across our way, a misplaced forest of many years' duration. It took us hours to find the road again. More often we crossed the bare earth left by the last rainstorm, leaving our footprints to mark our passage until the next rain washed them over. And there were other places where time and water had eroded the earth from under the roadway until, all support and strength gone, the roadbed had collapsed and left a deepening, widening gully to be crossed. A thin stream flowed through the bottom of one, and there we refreshed our water supply.

Hunting was plentiful and easy. The game in these areas had never seen nor heard of man, and often we came upon deer, raccoons, beaver, elk, bears, and goats (all easily identified for us by Avram) standing incuriously about as we approached them. Most often Avram would fit an arrow to his bow and bring an animal down, but sometimes, not to be outdone, I would make a throw with my knife for the day's meals. Certainly the supply of food was no problem, and we moved along the road more quickly than I had expected we would.

One night, after we had bedded ourselves down, I found myself restless and unable to fall asleep. Something, I knew, was bothering me, but I could not put a mental finger upon it. I was on the move again, and I should have been happy——happy as I had been before, when Rifka and I had been wending our own way north. It was a not unpleasant life. The road, with only enough exceptions to keep it interesting, was easy going. With Avram's help, hunting and cooking food was no problem, and occupied nowhere near the diversion of time it had before. But . . .

Rifka gave a breathy sigh and turned over, her rounded

haunches rubbing against my thigh. She seemed unusually fidgety herself, these days——or, rather, nights. She wriggled a little, settling herself closer to me. I wondered, in passing, why she continued to slip out of her clothes each night, instead of keeping them on, as Avram did, for greater warmth. I had suggested it to her, and on that occasion she had given me a strange look, then said only, "It's warmer this way," after insisting I remove my clothes too. I had. But it would soon be colder, and I wondered how long the bearskin could keep her warm enough.

I stared up into the sky. It was very black, the moon not yet risen. Overhead, the stars gleamed hard pinpricks in the fabric of night. As I watched, one of the moving stars slowly crossed the sky, east to west. It was a bright silver that faded before it disappeared beyond the hills to the west. It looked like the same one I had seen several nights earlier. Avram had pointed it out then, taking Rifka's arm and gesturing skyward. Our eyes had been blinded by the firelight, but the movement of the tiny dot of light against the fixed and immobile stars around it finally caught my eye.

The night breeze was a cool feather that glided over my face. I glanced at Rifka. Only the top of her head showed outside the cover of the skin. She was burrowed in for the night.

I felt awake. The air smelled magically good. The trees across the way whispered enticements to me. I wasn't really tired.

The fire was reduced to faintly glowing coals that brightened when the wind touched them. I stared across them at the dark bundle of Avram. It was unmoving, a cocoon of slumber. I thrust my arms out into the night air and stretched them. It felt good.

Slowly, careful not to disturb Rifka, I eased myself away from her, then slid out from under the skin. There was something special, something exciting, about standing erect in the cool darkness, alone and alive.

I drew on my leathers and my boots and, moving as soundlessly as I knew how, left the campsite.

I intended only a short walk, a prowl through the friendly night. I found myself thinking of myself as a nocturnal animal, and as I did, I touched my knife to assure myself it was there——and then smiled at myself.

It was a moment of magical make-believe, of fantasies and instincts. I followed the road west, in the direction we were heading, intending to go not far, but full of elation in myself. It was good to be alone again, to be unencumbered by the presence of, and responsibility for, others. Now I set my own pace, first running lightly across patches of grass and bare cracked concrete for a moment, then pausing to hold stock still while I listened to the call of some nearby but invisible night bird. My vision had adjusted to the dim light of the stars, and the roadway was a ghostly path of shades of gray; the overhanging trees deepening hues of greying black.

I saw a buck, up ahead, cantering along the roadway itself, head held high, antlers silhouetted against the sky before he crested the hill. *Aha!* I thought, and on silent slinking feet gave chase—not to make a needless kill, but for the sport of it.

The wind shifted, or the buck's ears were more finely tuned than I could imagine, for when I topped the hill, he was loping down the embankment and across a glade to the north and east, heading for the thin sickle of the rising moon.

I was grinning with joy as I followed him down, in a leap across the eroded drainage ditch and into the heavy grass. I felt myself a giant then, and a part of the very night herself. I ran on feet too fleet, the wind kissing my face, the grasses parting like magic under me.

The animal was faster, and he disappeared into the wall of trees before I was more than into the glade. But I marked the point of his disappearance, and when I found it, there was another trail to lead me on.

The light here was far dimmer, but my feet leapt over thrusting roots and bulking rock, and I ran down hill, over trickling stream, and up hill and on, the race an enchanted moment of forever *now*, excitement and joy buoying me upward and onward without thought to time or distance covered.

Then I saw the light ahead.

At first it seemed to wink on and off, beguilingly, will-othe-wispishly. Then the trees thinned, and I burst into a clearing, across which sat the little cottage.

It was nestled under the spreading arms of a gnarled and ancient oak. Its roof was dark, wood-shingled, but the neatly fitted frame siding was painted white, bright and startling in the forest night. Warm light spilled from the open doorway, outlining and silhouetting two figures.

One was a buck, a tall, proud animal which turned its head to look back over its shoulders at me, and then moved quietly and without haste out of the light and into the blackness of the forest beyond.

The other was an old man. He was short, shorter even than Rifka, but very stout, and white hair fell from his head to his shoulders, a white beard full against his chest. He was wearing clothing which I found myself recognizing——as I had recognized the new and strange before: a dark tweed vest over a white shirt, sleeves rolled to the elbows, dark trousers, also tweed, and large scuffed brown slippers.

His eyes seemed to twinkle as he stepped back into the room beyond the doorway, more fully into the light. "Come in, come in, young man," he called out, gesturing to me.

Unbelievingly, I crossed the threshold. I had to stoop to enter; the doorway was cut too low. The room inside seemed to be the only one in the cottage. Along a near wall, a fire burned merrily in a stone fireplace. Across from it was an old easy chair. A shaded lamp burned on a tall stand set just behind and to one side of it. Beside the chair was a table, and, across the far wall were shelves and cupboards. By the fireplace were hung pots and pans and other cooking utensils. The floorboards were wide planks of oak, stained by age and polished by use. In front of the chair was a fur rug, a warm rich brown. Overhead, the rafters were naked beams, and shadowy objects were hung from them. Close by the door, and unnoticed until I was in the room, were two straight chairs of fashioned wood.

"Well, now, I certainly am glad you came by," the old man said. His voice was rusty with age, but cheerful and firm. "Please sit down." He gestured at one of the straight chairs. "Won't you have something to drink?" He moved to the fireplace and drew from one side a kettle. He ladled into two black iron mugs something that even across the small room smelled fragrantly spicy and warm. He carried them back, and handed one to me, settling with the other into the easy chair. Numbly, I grasped the mug's handle and let myself down, jerkily, into a chair.

"Let me introduce myself," he said. "I am Tom Greenwood." He beamed at me, then raised his mug in a salute.

"I'm, uh, Tanner," I said. I took a sip from my mug. It was hot. The stuff kindled a warmth that slid down into me while its sweet taste lingered in my mouth. "What is this?"

He made a sound that was half chuckle, half a throat-clearing grunt. "Ah, you like it, then? Mulled cider, it is, and my very own recipe, too. Good for a brisk evening, and those to follow as well, I can assure you. Bracing and healthy. Tanner what? Is that your first name or your last?"

"I don't know. It's just my name."

"Ahh. I see. You don't know." His brows furrowed, eyes narrowing for a moment. Then he shrugged. "Strange," he muttered. "Oh, well." He looked up again, his cheery mood seemingly restored.

"You came from the Old Road," he said. It seemed both statement and question.

"Yes," I said. "How'd you know?"

He chuckled again. "Old Alron told me. He led you a merry chase."

" 'Old Alron'?" I echoed. My mind was churning. Somehow I could not believe this could be real. There was a dreamlike quality to it all. "You don't mean——?"

"The stag? Why, yes. He caught your scent first, then when he saw you, he decided to bring you to me. It's very unusual, you know, when a man chances along the Old Road. He knew I was lonesome for the company of men."

"You, ah, *spoke* with the deer?" I asked.

He chuckled again. "Not as you and I speak, no. But, yes, we spoke." He let his breath out in a long sigh. "Living here in the forest as I do, I have scant contact with men. My most frequent visitors are the dwellers of the forest themselves. Still . . ." He looked up at me then, over the top of his mug, his eyes suddenly intent. "Still, I wonder now. *Are* you a man?"

A chill passed over me, and the iron of the mug felt alien in my fingers.

73

"What makes you ask that?" I returned.

"It's a curious thing," he said, more musing to himself than replying directly to me. "There was a time when the Death Machine sent its emissaries out through the world. Could one possibly be left, do you think, still roaming about?" Again, that sharp look: "Declare yourself. Man, or machine?"

I put down the mug. My fingers crawled to be free of it. "Explain yourself," I said, still unwilling to make a direct answer. "It strikes me you're far more of an oddity than I. What are you doing here, alone in the forest, living in a little house the likes of which are unknown today, wearing clothing that dates from . . ." I started to say *before my own time* before my tongue stumbled on the words and I caught myself short. "You're an anomaly," I said quickly. "You don't belong here at all."

He upended his mug, draining it, then let it thump to the table between us. "Interesting. That's interesting. Tell me: what are men doing now, out in the world beyond?"

I turned the question over in my mind. "They live a primitive life. Some live it as savages, spending their lives in squalid surroundings, raiding their fellows, and hunting each other as game, cannibals. Others have struggled back into villages, hunt, garden for the common benefit of the village. They scavenge among the ruins for building materials; they dress as I am dressed."

He nodded. "You've borrowed their clothes. What of your own?"

"I have none of my own."

"You lost them? They rotted with age? What?"

"You never answered *my* questions."

"True. But you've answered mine."

"How? What do you mean?"

He leaned back, and gestured at me. "I sensed it when you entered. You don't carry the, ah, aura of mankind. There is something, I should guess, of the tragic about you . . . doomed to wander the earth forever, until your batteries, or whatever, run down. How many centuries, now? What do you do, in these times of decay? There is nothing left, you know. Your purposes have long been taken care of. You should have been recalled, dismantled, destroyed——*destroyed as you yourself have destroyed!*" He

74

was leaning forward now, sparks all but shooting from his eyes. He seemed taller, bigger suddenly.

I found myself wanting to escape his penetrating gaze, his pointing finger. But anger was building within me, an anger that made me want to answer him, to shout back at him.

"Batteries?" I interrupted, "centuries? What in hell are you talking about? I don't know what it is you think I am, but you're wrong, whatever it is. I——"

"You want to know what I think you are?" he said, rising to his feet. He seemed to tower over me. "You *know* what I think you are. I know you for what you are, one of the spawn of the Death Machine! You're a robot, built in the form of Man, built to spew death, programmed to sow destruction upon the Earth!"

"*No!*" Now I was shouting as I rose to my feet to confront him. Now I was the taller, and he fell back. "No, you're wrong!"

But, a voice in my mind insidiously inquired, *is he?*

CHAPTER TEN

With an agility I would not have expected of him, the old man leapt to the fireplace, seized a knife from its place on the wall, and came at me with it.

I could not react. I felt frozen in my boots, locked to the floor. I watched, some part of my mind squirming in horror, as he threw himself at me, knife thrusting, shouting, "I'll prove it, *I'll prove it,* you tin box!"

For a moment my muscles slackened, and I threw up my arm. The knife slashed across my forearm. It sank suddenly and quickly to the bone, the jar racing up to my shoulder. Blood spurted into the air as the knife came free, its blade stained dark crimson.

Tom Greenwood stared at me in horror, the knife slipping from his grasp to thud against the wooden floor. His hand flew to his mouth. "Oh, my God," he said, over and over. "Oh, my God, oh, my God, oh, my God . . ."

In that distant, unblinking part of my mind that was always sane and always questioning, I wondered, *why didn't I react as I did before?* Why hadn't my metabolism speeded up, allowing me to evade the blow? Or, failing that, why hadn't I somehow burned my attacker, as I had the bear?

The old man had torn a sheet into ribbons, and now, his fingers shaking and fumbling in his hurry, he wrapped them around my wounded arm, muttering as he did, "The knife was clean; that'll help. And the cut was clean. If we keep it bound, it shouldn't bleed too much. You shouldn't lose too much blood. There, now . . . You better sit down . . . here, the good chair . . . rest yourself. Liquids, that's what we need now, lots of liquids. That's right, ease back. Keep your arm up on the arm of the chair; I'll refill your mug. Oh, my God, my God, my God . . ."

His easy chair was soft and comfortable. Black spots passed briefly before my eyes, then cleared as he held the mug for me to sip from. The cider was soothing in my throat, and a fresh breeze through my brain.

He sat again, this time on the edge of the chair in which I'd been sitting. He leaned forward, eyes worried. "You must forgive me," he said. "Please forgive me. I—I became carried away . . . not myself."

"I don't understand," was all I could bring myself to say.

"I've lived too long alone, I guess," he said. "My mind . . . . I guess I'm not all I once was. I, well, I was wrong about you. I still don't understand. . ." He wrung his hands. "But I *was* wrong."

"What," I asked, "did you expect?"

"If you'd been a robot," he said, shaking his head, "well, I don't know, but you wouldn't have bled." He leaned over and picked up the knife. It had fallen near the heat of the fireplace. The blade was crusted black. "It wouldn't have been blood," he said.

"These robots," I said. "What were they?"

"They were before your day, Tanner," he said. "Terrible machines that looked like men, but which tore down the civilization of men. They destroyed the cities and drove men out to suffer, naked, in the countryside——to die. They tore it all down. Look."

He stood up and went to the shelves. They were filled with books, all very old and worn-looking. He pulled one from its shelf and brought it back. "The diary of my ancestor," he explained, opening it and showing it to me. Its lined pages were filled with the faded scrawl of handwriting. I squinted at it in the dim light.

"Aghh," he said, snapping it shut, "I forgot. Reading is a lost art." He flipped it open again, then began thumbing through its pages. "Ah, ummm . . . here: 'June 5th—I find myself writing this entry with numbed fingers. I guess it started with the teevee this morning. I'd tuned it in as all sane citizens do, while eating breakfast. Dora was still in the kitchen. I wasn't really watching it though—not really listening, anyway—when Dora said something was wrong with our kitchen faucet. There wasn't any more water coming out. Just then the teevee caught my attention, when they made the announcement. The screen showed a group of Proctors lined up in a row, and then, while I watched, *right while I watched,* they shot the entire line of Proctors down. They *killed* them. I was stunned. Dora had come out from the kitchen because I hadn't come in to check the faucet, and she said, "Isn't that Ed Bagley?" One of the men they killed was Ed Bagley from down in 46-GG, just

77

two floors down. I guess that made it really real. And then they made the announcement, and all over again, I just couldn't believe it. In one half hour all services would be off, they said. The water was already off. The upstate aqueducts had been blown up. No more water for the city! And they'd be destroying the power stations in a half hour. No more teevee. No more brain-scanners. No more Proctors. Chaos. That's what they said, there would be Chaos. I don't think I really believed it all then. I guess I thought it was some sort of very un-sane joke. And Dora said, "What about the elevators? Hadn't we better use them while we can?" But I don't like that. It makes no sense. Where would we *go*? Dora says we've got to get out of the City, that it will be impossible to live here. I just don't know. Sam Fellows came over this afternoon, after the power went off, and we talked about it. It was while he was still here that we heard the screams, from out in the hall, and Mrs. Fellows came in a moment later to say that a gang of some sort was breaking into apartments two floors down. Mildred diPreto had just come up to warn her, and had gotten slashed with a knife. We barricaded the door with furniture, but I guess the gangs had had enough of climbing stairs. We never did see them on this floor. Dinner was a mess. No heat for the stove, and the fridge thawing out. Dora wanted to use everything that would spoil, but raw steak (we'd been saving it in the freezer for something special) and raw thawed vegetables . . . well, just not my idea of a meal. We finally made a fire with crumpled toilet paper in the big frying pan and ate half-raw, half-burnt steaks. It was better than nothing, but I'm not looking forward to raw eggs tomorrow. ——Oh, Dora just read this and told me we'd be having eggnog, which is okay, I guess. It's funny looking out the window tonight. No lights. A few people like us have flashlights, I guess, but I'm used to seeing the lighted-up windows in the next complex over, and about all I can see now——hold it. There seems to be a fire, about a quarter mile away. Christ, yes! It's just burst through the roof of the Tenth Avenue Complex, and now it's lighting up the sky! Low clouds, bouncing the light back. Wow! I sure hope nothing like that gets started in this building! Sam's here as I write this, staring out the window and cursing. It strikes me as the work of one of those gangs. We've seen them down in the streets. But Sam is convinced it's another step toward Chaos, and deliberately planned by what he is now calling the Death Machine. It's funny how times can change so fast. Only yesterday there was a documentary on the teevee about it, and about how wonderful it was, monitoring all the brain-scanners and everything, and now Sam calls it the Death Machine. And I guess he's right. I wonder what we can *do*.' "

The old man's voice had grown hoarse. He got up and refilled his own mug, took a long draught, then grunted with satisfaction. He picked the book up again, and thumbed forward a few pages.

" 'June 9th—Dora died today. I can't say I'm surprised. The new life was just too tough on her. Yesterday we had to do all that running, when the farmer saw us and began shooting. She wasn't young. She didn't feel well this ayem. Sleeping in wet grass didn't help either. And today it is still raining. This morning, we were surprised by a gang of Rovers, and we had to run again. This time I didn't mind firing back, but there were too many of them to fight it out with. Our food has been gone for three days. Who can say what finally did it to her? It was still light, and still raining this afternoon when Dora told me, "I just can't go on." Then she fell down and died. A stroke? Hunger? Exposure? I just don't know. I tried to bury her, but a few eating utensils aren't much to dig a grave with, and I'm no longer a young man myself. I ended up covering her up with stones. Thank God—if He's still around—for New York State stone fences. At least the stones were plentiful. I laid her under a fence and pushed it over on her. I hope the animals don't get her too quickly. It isn't right. And now I have to figure what I'm going to do with myself. The best thing I can think of, now that I'm alone, is to get up to the summer cottage, by the lake. It's probably been plundered by now, and maybe people are in it, but I'll cross that bridge when I get to it. I have a gun—a good old-fashioned Colt revolver—and I don't think I'll mind as much using it now. ——Later: I had to move on and find better shelter. They're patrolling in helicopters again, and my chosen spot for the night was unfortunately open to the sky. Oh, well, at least it isn't raining any more. I wish this tree didn't drip so badly; I'm afraid my ink will run. Damned foolish of me.

Those demons! If I thought it would do any good, I'd try shooting one down. But they're indestructible, and I'm not, so best I don't call attention to myself.' " He looked up at me. "Those seem like representative passages."

"What happened to him?" I asked.

"The diary stops just a few pages further on," the old man said. "But he escaped. And he took a second wife and sired a son."

I looked around. "You have no son," I said. "Will the line end here?"

He shook his head and chuckled. The sound of it was reassuring. "I have a son. He'll return when it's time."

"How will he know?"

"He'll know. We always know." He frowned. "Except about you . . ."

"There's always one of you here," I said. It wasn't really a question. I sensed it was true.

He nodded. "Yes," he said. He climbed to his feet, and went to the door. "Getting late. I'll give you my bed for the night."

"Your bed?" I asked. "I don't see one."

He closed the door and went over to the cupboards. He opened a tall narrow door. "I keep it put away when it's not needed," he said. He reached in, and, wheezing, swung a bed out edgewise, pivoted it around, and lowered it to the floor. It was the first real bed I'd seen.

"No," I said. "Thanks, but you keep it. I've got to be going."

"Going? Going where?" His tone was sharp.

"I wasn't traveling alone. My companions are camped back on the roadway. They're asleep, but I don't want them to wake up and find me gone. They won't know where I am, what happened to me."

"Your companions?"

"A girl from among the savages, and a man from one of the villages."

"What are they to you? Why do you travel with them?" he asked.

"The girl is . . . well, my responsibility, I guess. She's very young. I took her from a tribe that had captured her. The man is just a fellow traveler, out to see the world, as I am. I don't know how long he'll stay with us."

"Where are you bound?"

"West. I don't know how far. Do you know what lies beyond these hills?"

His brow wrinkled. "Mountains, to begin with. Beyond them, the great plains, and, far to the west, more mountains. They're far higher, much worse. And, beyond them, another ocean. As for people . . . You'll not find many this side of the mountains, but beyond them . . . well, not everyone suffered as much as the others. There are people. Some of them . . . I don't know. You'll see for yourself. But you'll find people."

"Why haven't you gone to them?" I asked.

He smiled. It was a tired smile, and it was then I realized how very old indeed he was. "I've been there, once, long ago."

I stood up. I felt dizzy for a moment, and my arm began throbbing with my pulse, but it passed, and then I felt stronger.

"Here, now," the old man cried out in alarm. "Do you think you really should?" I couldn't tell if he was genuinely concerned, or simply wanted to keep my company for as long as he might. I sensed that much time had already passed.

"I must," I said.

"You mustn't think badly of me for what I did," he said in a low voice. It was as close as he came to begging me.

"No," I said, moving to the door. "I don't. You were a help, in other ways."

"A help?" he asked, brightening.

"You've explained a great deal to me—about the, uh, cataclysm or whatever."

"The Chaos," he said. "The work of the Death Machine."

"Yeah."

"Goodbye," he said.

"Goodbye," I said, and closed the door behind me.

The fresh night air felt cold against my skin, and it shocked me a little bit, like ducking my head in a mountain stream. I stared back at the closed door of the cottage, and at the improbable little house itself. Chinks of light spilled out from under the door and around its sides. Suddenly, a shower of sparks leapt out of the low chimney. Then the light disappeared.

It was almost as though it had never happened, as though the old man didn't even exist. Except for my throbbing arm. I glanced up at the stars. The moon was almost at the western tree-line. I started across the little clearing, hunting for the trail I'd followed.

It was slow going, on the return. The trail seemed to have many dips and twists that I didn't remember, and I stumbled frequently on exposed roots, while low branches seemed to be reaching out to pull at my clothes or whip suddenly across my face. The light was worse than useless. It formed weird and distractingly deceptive patterns on the trail, deep shadows concealing hollows, brighter patches overlaying sudden upthrustings of rock.

I walked and I walked. There seemed to be no end to the trail. Twice I came to branching cross-trails of which I had no memory. I tried to keep due-west.

I stumbled and fell too frequently. The last time it happened, a sudden branch tore at the wrappings of my wound, ripping them apart. The cloth was old. It tore easily. And no piece was left long enough to wrap completely around my arm. But the wound didn't seem to want to come open again, so I left it unwrapped. The air might be good for it.

Finally I came out into the glade. Ahead I could see the embankment of the roadway. It was a welcome sight.

I glanced up into the sky. The moon was gone. To the east the sky was greyed and growing lighter. It was nearly dawn. Where had my night gone? I was exhausted, and I'd had no sleep! For once, I welcomed the idea of curling up against Rifka's firm little body. The night air was chilly and I missed the warmth of Tom Greenwood's fire.

As I wearily climbed the road up the hill I'd raced down long hours ago, I found myself reacting as though to a strange and troubling dream. Or was it flatly a nightmare? How much could I really believe, now, in looking back over those already oddly distant memories? So much had happened . . . and so little of it really made sense.

Every bone in my body ached as I trudged down the hill toward the distant shapes of our campsite. Tired: bone tired. I was more tired than I'd been in many weeks. What was it I'd started out for? A stroll to make me sleepy? Well, it had done that, all right. That, and a little more. My arm only ached, now, one ache among many. When I touched it, it felt hot, but firm. I wondered what the old man would've made of that. I knew damned well I healed faster than humans. Would he have decided I was one of those demon robots after all? I shivered. The cold was eating into me, following hard on my fatigue. The bearskin, Rifka's warm little body to cuddle against, and sleep—any sleep at all. That's what I wanted. That would be just fine. I forced the anticipation to lift each foot and put it down again a step ahead, as I trudged down the last slope. It would be morning all too soon, and I didn't want to see it before I fell asleep . . .

The campsite looked wrong.

The greying dawn washed out contrasts. The stars were dim now, the moon gone. It was hard to make out the details, but something . . . I couldn't place my finger on it . . . something was different . . . wrong.

Then I was closer. Then I could see. And hear.

The bearskin, closest to me as I approached, lay flat. Unoccupied.

Across the black smudge of the dead fire, Avram's bedding looked strangely bulky.

And it was moving.

I felt something cold and dead form in the pit of my stomach. My head seemed very far away from my feet. I was weirdly detached from the scene I was viewing.

The sounds were monotonously regular; I'd heard grunts like these before——long before.

I found myself standing just beyond the bearskin, unmoving, frozen, and unwilling witness to all that would, inevitably, happen.

The movements in the rolled bedding grew more violent. A low wild moan began in jerky gasps. It built slowly, into a ululating shriek that climaxed in a muffled scream. But not of pain. The pain was twisting itself within my gut.

Then came a deeper groan, and a masculine snort of pleasure.

The movement stopped.

CHAPTER ELEVEN

The expression on Avram's face was wooden, but a curious malice seemed to show through his eyes. His tone was neutral, though, as he said, "I'll be back." He moved quickly down the embankment and into the trees.

Rifka looked at me with searching eyes. "You were gone, you know," she said. "I didn't know you'd come back."

I felt cold and bleak. I was consumed by emotions I didn't know I possessed. I shook my head. I wondered why we were talking about it. I'd had perhaps two hours of sleep, before Rifka's startled exclamation had awakened me. I'd rolled myself in the bearskin without removing my clothes, cold and miserably tired, and my eyes had burned when I'd closed them. I had not slept well. When Rifka discovered my return, it had awakened me quickly. But she had said nothing, and I had said nothing——until now.

"I woke up and I was cold," she said. "You were gone. I saw the stars, and it was very late. I thought—I thought you had gone away. Your clothes were gone, your boots, your knife." Her voice was low and husky, and she seemed to be forcing herself to speak. "So I went to Avram. I wanted to be warm."

"It was more than that," I said at last.

Color flamed in her face. "Yes," she said, with sudden heat. "It was more than that. I needed a man. Do you blame me? Can you blame me for that? For how long now have I slept with you and waited? 'Why don't we keep our clothes on?' you said"——her tone was scornful as she parroted me—"but Avram was willing to take his off when I joined him. Avram is a man."

"And I am not," I finished it for her.

Suddenly, inexplicably, tears sprang into her eyes. "You, Tanner——what *are* you?"

I shook my head and did not answer.

"Where *were* you, then?" she asked, after wiping her arm across her eyes. Her voice steadied.

"I don't know whether you would believe me," I said. "I couldn't sleep. I got up to walk. I found a cottage in the wood, and an old man, who told me about how Chaos came . . ."

The words meant too little to her.

"The dead cities—this road." I kicked at it. "How do you think it all happened? Why did it all happen?"

"I dunno," she answered. "Does it matter?"

"Aren't you curious?" I asked.

"Not very. Not about that. It's done. It happened long ago. It doesn't matter any more. Other things matter."

"Yes, I suppose they do . . ."

Then Avram was climbing back up toward us. He nodded at me. "Didn't expect you back," he said.

Sudden anger bridled within me. "You didn't?"

"It doesn't matter. It won't change things," he said.

"How's that?" I asked.

"Rifka," he said. "She sleeps with me now."

I stared at him. His eyes left mine.

"What does it matter to you?" he asked. "You did nothing for her. We could all see it. It was her choice; she made it."

I turned toward Rifka; she was bending over, her back to us, remaking the packs. She kept busied, saying nothing.

I nodded. "Okay," I said. And in that moment I had never felt more distant from the human race.

It was an unpleasant day, strangely overcast, the winds bringing a clammy cold down off the hillslopes. As we passed the glade I'd crossed the night before, I tried to pick out the place where the trail opened into the woods. I couldn't find it. Even the glade looked different. I had said nothing more about my nocturnal adventure. Indeed, no one had spoken further, except as was necessary in making the morning meal, and in packing. Rifka had stayed apart from us both, her eyes downcast, her expression closed. Only Avram seemed to be enjoying himself very much, and even he did not seem as happy as he might have expected to be.

That night I killed a goat, and we roasted it, lingering over the meal, which included tubers buried in the coals of the fire until they were roasted, and small pungent bulbs which Avram had found and we ate raw. They made our breaths stink.

Finally it could be put off no longer. We unrolled our bedding. I sat down on the bearskin, unwilling to do more. Avram eagerly peeled off his leather tunic, exposing a sinewy, leather-skinned chest and torso, and then bent to pull off his leggings.

Rifka had not spoken at all during the meal. Now she gazed at the fire, her back to us, as if undecided, or just putting off the inevitable. The backs of my hands felt prickly, and I clenched and unclenched them only half aware that I was doing it.

Avram slipped into his skins, but did not roll up in them. He flashed me a sharp, mocking glance. In disgust, I climbed, fully clothed, into the bearskin, and pulled it tight around me.

I didn't want to look at them, but I couldn't make myself look away. Rifka climbed slowly to her feet, her face hidden in the flickering shadows, the fire lapsing now into embers. Then, still clothed, she bent down and crawled into Avram's bedding. I closed my eyes then, and, my stomach clenching in spasms, forced myself into an unpleasantly dreamless sleep.

I didn't like to face these things in myself. Yet, they must be faced. I was not a human. Yet, I was passing myself off as a human. Only Rifka truly knew some of my inhuman attributes. (I'd said nothing of the knife slashing; only a thin line marked my arm that day. And it ached seldom. A clean cut, as Greenwood had said, and quickly healing.)

And yet . . . what were these emotions I was suffering, if not human emotions. Where was the line to be drawn? Old Greenwood had sensed I was not a man. And Rifka had said it: she needed a man. Avram had seen it; I'd seen it myself, without wanting to recognize it. Her moods, her restlessness, her readiness to sleep so intimately with me. I should have remembered: she'd long been no virgin. Why had I assumed it had always been against her will? *She was human, wasn't she?*

And I wasn't.

It always came back to that. What was I, that I had been

sent out into the world of men, sheathed in the aspects of Man, inoculated with even the feelings of a man, but yet *not* a man?

There was too much about me that I did not know. And now I was falling into my own personal maelstrom of Chaos.

The next day, as we followed the road westward into the real mountains, I made my decision. I would leave them. Rifka no longer needed me; she wasn't my responsibility any longer. Avram would be happy to look after her. And, for reasons I was unsure of, I no longer wanted their company. Somewhere inside me there was an ache that started up again each time I saw them together. I tried to remember my elation when I'd broken free on that night of adventure. It had been like casting off weights I hadn't known I was carrying. I tried to feel the same lightness in anticipation. But it didn't come.

That day had been another dreary one, the low clouds overhead threatening rain at any moment, but never breaking. The night was damp and chill, and we built up a good fire. It was a night for huddling close for mutual warmth. As I saw Rifka and Avram climbing into their bedding across the fire, it hardened my resolve. I would wait until they were asleep, and then go. I needed no more prodding.

The concrete under my bearskin was flat and hard and cold. The skin was stiff, and the chill penetrated through it as though I was lying on bare ground. I fidgeted in my desire to be up and moving. I pulled the skin up over my head, burrowing into it for what little comfort it might give me, and waited. I dozed, despite myself. When I snapped suddenly and guiltily awake, the campsite was silent, the fire dead. The night was black. I had to strain my eyes to see the huddled mass that was Avram and Rifka.

With unaccustomed stealth, I climbed to my feet. A wind had come up. It cut through me, and I wanted to jump and clap my hands to limber up and warm myself. But I didn't. I gathered the bearskin, and stowed it in my pack, leaving the other items I'd been carrying—most of them Avram's excess baggage—in a neat pile on the road. I would carry no food. Only my bearskin—*I'd* killed it, after all—my knife, my fire-maker, and a water-skin. The bearskin filled the pack anyway, and it made a bulky load when I got it onto my shoulders.

I stood still for a moment and tried to peer through the murky night at the dark shape where Rifka lay. But I could see nothing that I could identify as her. No hair, no hand, no face.

There would be no goodbye.

Silently I left them and turned westward, to follow the dim outline of the road deeper into the mountains.

I made the trek without event for the next week. I had no fear they'd catch up to me, and little confidence they'd want to. I moved far more quickly now. I ate only once— and noticed that in skipping meals I utilized the bulk of what I did eat to a far greater extent. Hunger pangs struck the end of my first day, after hiking continuously all through the night and day, but did not last. I had been pampering myself, fitting myself to *human* needs and standards. Now I was free again.

But lonely.

The days were monotonously overcast, the clouds a continuing threat that was never delivered. As I moved up into the mountains, the grey ceiling dropped closer, never breaking. The days were very empty. I filled them by walking, my pace brisk and steady. I knew I was covering the ground at twice the speed that Avram and Rifka would. Often I walked well into the night, and, when I was too cold to sleep long, I would rise before dawn to start on again.

As the second week began, the long-held rain began falling, first in a drizzle, then, on the second day, in torrents. When the rain got too heavy, I found a shallow cave in a cliff overhanging the road and retreated there. I made a fire of pine wood, and built it up into a roaring blaze, letting my leathers steam dry on me so that they wouldn't shrink too badly. I waited until the rain was a drizzle again, and then, the bearskin a cloak over my head and shoulders, I pushed on. There were few if any people in these mountains, Old Tom Greenwood had said, but many lived beyond. I wanted to get over these mountains, and put them behind me. I needed something new with which to fill my existence.

PART THREE

CHAPTER TWELVE

"Up with your hands, there!" rang out the voice. It was sharp and firm, the voice of a man who was very certain of himself. "Get 'em up, or I'll shoot you down."

I raised my hands, scanning as I did so the heavy growth of trees to each side of the narrow road.

"Okay, Now move on up where we can get a look at you," the unseen voice said.

I'd left the big road when it turned north again. I'd passed several intersections of the big road with other roads, but most of these had been north-south roads, and of no interest to me. The intersections were curiously graded, though, massive embankments leading up to places where once great bridges must have spanned. Now only a little rust remained, and sometimes it hadn't been easy to find the way on across the interchanges. This smaller road had crossed under the road I'd been following, and had wound its way westward into the low mountains. The main road had turned in a great curve due north, and I could see no change in its course for as far as it remained in sight—a good distance up the valley it followed. I had decided to leave it, to continue west.

The day was, like most of the days now, cloudy. Grey banks scudded across the sky. When the sun broke through, it was only for moments at a time. The winds were out of the north—they swept down the valley in heavy gusts—and the trees were shedding their leaves, while the mountains turned rainbow colors. The road was following a narrow gap in the mountains, the road itself choked with undergrowth and often no wider than a few feet. I'd been hoping it wouldn't play out. Thick pine and spruce grew along the gap, filling the crisp air with the heavy scent of resin. Now low green boughs were thrust aside, and men

89

came at me from each side of the road. One of them was pointing a long-barreled object at me, and once more my subconscious mental catalogue supplied a name: *Rifle——gun*.

"You alone?" the man with the gun asked.

I nodded. "What do you want with me?" I returned.

A couple of others had come up from behind me. I'd walked into a trap. The mountains weren't *quite* empty of people.

"Mebbe nothing, mebbe something," he replied. "Depends."

He was a scrawny little man, his Adam's apple jutting from his neck almost as protuberantly as his hawk nose. His eyes were black and beady and jumped about nervously. His hair was black, flecked with grey, and close-cropped. He needed a shave, but wore no beard or mustache. His clothes were of roughly woven cloth, and hung upon him as if made for someone else entirely.

"Don't get many strangers along this road," he added.

The other man was taller, heavier, but had the same darting black eyes, the same ill-fitting clothing. His jaws worked, and then he spat a brown stream at the ground. He said nothing.

"How is it you were expecting me, then?" I asked.

The man with the gun gave a hacking laugh. "Ol' Jed here, he was up on the moun-tane, and he saw yuh a-coming." He slung his thumb at the one chewing his cud without letting his rifle waver an inch.

"I'm just a traveler," I said. "I've never been here before. I mean you no harm."

"And I reckon you'll do us none——one way or t'other, the little man said. "But we ain't a hard lot to get along with. You prove out, and you'll get on okay." He nodded in the direction I'd been traveling. "Let's get a move on."

I fell into line behind Ol' Jed and one of the others, who, from the back, was indistinguishable. The man with the gun was behind me, and somebody else, once addressed as "Glenn," brought up the rear.

The growth of pine grew heavier, crowding into the road from each side until a man could barely slip through. I saw why I'd been stopped where I was: along here it would have been too easy for me to jump into the trees, and too difficult to pin me down as I had been, back in the open. But my man with the gun was only a few steps behind me, and I had no real desire to break free now. I was more interested in seeing where they were leading me.

The road had degenerated into a narrow trail, but as we crossed a clearing, I glanced up to see the mountain gap behind us. And soon the trail was descending. When it broke free of the trees at last, it did so suddenly, and I beheld my first real town.

No thrown-up village, this. It was once the site of Mercer, Pennsylvania, I was told, and a new town, called New Mercer, had been built over its ruins, following roughly its street plans, in the last fifty years.

It was a self-sufficient community, dependent upon farming and hunting, and with its own curious industries, fiercely suspicious of strangers—as all self-contaned communities seemed to be so far—but friendly enough in its fashion, nonetheless.

There was no wall around the town, and the houses were simple, but well-built of frame and brick. The streets were paved with bricks, and oxen pulled heavy wagons in a slow plod while horses with light drays danced around them.

"Who's going to make the decision about me?" I asked, as we descended the slope for the town.

"Don't you fret on it," came the reply from behind me.

I was marched along the side of a wide street past houses and then small barnlike buildings from which sometimes came clanking, hammering sounds. The street was not heavily trafficked, but it was still noisy. An ox-drawn wagon, for instance, would make a tremendous din as it passed. The ox was shod, and its lugubrious shuffle was a clatter in and of itself. But the rumble of iron-tired wheels on the pavement, and the squeal of wooden hubs turning on wooden axles, all but drowned the ox out. And of course no ox-driver would be content to sit on his high box without adding his voice to the din. "Hi, there, you Blue Bell! Gawddammit, git *on* with ye!" And a short whip would pop over the placid animal's flanks, perhaps startling a few flies. It did not take many wagons to fill the street with noise.

No one stopped or paused to peer at us as we made our

way along the sides of the streets, dodging piles of dung and hasty horsemen. The two in front of me were now walking abreast, and I supposed those behind were doing the same. We made a compact group, but not, it would seem, an unusual one.

We came to the town square. A dozen streets emptied into the block-long, two-block-wide square, in the center of which was a park, trees, and a small grandstand. Our destination was on the near side of the square, an imposing looking building three stories in height.

"This here's our Town Hall," my captor said. "And I reckon the Mayor's in."

"He most always is, this time of the day," said Glenn with a weak laugh.

The Mayor was a man who looked like he'd never left his oversized chair. He was constructed like a pyramid, his bald dome narrow and pointed, an island rising above the sea of fluffy grey hair, his ears wide fleshy flaps, his nose a shapeless bulge, his grizzled cheeks pouching out into overflowing jowls. He had no neck; his jowls rested on his sloping shoulders. His paunch was the bottom of the pyramid. He looked like a sack of sand left in one place too long, everything settled into the bottom. His hands were laced together across his stomach, which was as handy a place as any, I guess, for resting them. His eyes were closed.

"Ahh, Mister Mayor!" It was the first time I'd heard Ol' Jed speak.

The Mayor's eyes opened wide. His eyes were big. They were wide-set and bulged. They looked like the eyes of a deer I'd killed once, brown and liquid and innocent. They totally changed the man's appearance.

His voice was high-pitched, like a boy's, but he spoke softly. "Jed, Glenn, Mark, Peter . . ." He inclined his head a fraction, in a nod that acknowledged them. "Problem?"

"Got a man heah," my man with the gun said. Mark, he was. "Picked him up on the Eastern Road, at the gap."

"'Cause you any trouble?"

"Nope," he shook his head emphatically. "None."

The Mayor raised his limpid eyes to mine. "What's your name?"

"Tanner," I said.

He looked me up and down. "What's your business?"

I shrugged. "Traveler, I guess."

"You *guess?*"

"I travel."

"Where you traveling to?"

"West."

"And where from?"

"East."

He snorted. "Well, that takes it all in." His eyes closed. Nobody moved. His lips began working, doing a strange fleshy dance of their own, pushing in and out. I wondered what he was supposed to be doing.

His eyes snapped open again and looked directly up at me. "What do you have to say for yourself?"

"What do you want?" I asked, a little exasperated by this whole charade. "I'm a wanderer, out to see the country. I'm headed west. West meant your Eastern road, through the gap. And that brought me here. I've made no trouble about your men here holding me up at gunpoint; I'm a peaceable man. About all that I want is to have done with all this and go on about my way."

"You know," the Mayor said, his voice reflective, "to look at this town, it's a pretty good sized town by all accounts, and you'd think it was pretty full up with people.

"It isn't." His pudgy fingers climbed into a steeple. It was a cute trick. "We don't get nasty about it, but we like to try to convince travelers to stay."

"Maybe, without getting nasty about it, I don't *want* to stay."

The Mayor's eyes leaned to my left. "Mark. Put down the rabbit rifle and go get Margot."

"Yessir." He leaned the gun in the corner and went through another door.

"We have, ummm, inducements," the Mayor said, his eyes returning to me. "Not nasty at all."

Margot was a slender young woman whose age I estimated to be early or mid-twenties. She wore her black hair in a long braid that fell almost to her waist. Her dress was as homespun as the other clothing I'd seen on the people here, but it fit her. Her eyes were large, black, and softly glowing. They were fixed on me.

"Margot is my daughter," the Mayor said. "She acts as my secretary, as my, ahh, emissary. She would enjoy showing you about New Mercer. I'd like you to see a little more of it before you make up your mind. Please?"

My directive? *Go out into the world of men*——? They weren't holding me now. I was supposed to move among men——not empty forests. I nodded.

Margot smiled.

"This is Tanner, my dear," the Mayor told her. "Please treat him well." He closed his eyes, dismissing us.

The girl seemed shy at first, speaking very formally, as though guiding me on a set tour. But when she found I hadn't eaten yet this day, her reserve seemed to break, and she insisted I come with her to her house for a meal.

"You don't live with your father, your parents?" I asked.

"My mother is dead. The Mayor rarely leaves his office. I take his meals to him."

"Do you have to show many strangers like me around for him?" I asked.

She flushed. "Not—not many, ah, like you, no," she said in sudden confusion. I wondered what it was I'd said.

Her house was small; two rooms downstairs, two upstairs. It was boxed in between two other houses on a treelined side street. The kitchen was the second room on the lower floor. She opened the back door and went down three steps into a garden, where she picked herbs and spices. These went into a pot in which meat and vegetables were already simmering slowly. The smells were very good. I counted back the days and decided I was ready for another meal anyway.

We ate from wooden plates with cupped sides. The table was narrow, and we sat across from each other, our knees almost touching. I watched her use her spoon and imitated her movements until I had the feel of it. The stew was thick and hearty, full of flavors I could not identify. I ate three dishes full, while she watched, in silence.

Finally, when I leaned back from the table, she laughed. "You have quite an appetite, Tanner!"

"It was my first meal of the day," was all I said.

She laughed again. "All that walking . . . I'm worn out.

Aren't you?" Her eyes seemed to dance with an inner delight. When she smiled, I decided, she was very attractive. She didn't take after her father at all.

She glanced out the kitchen window. The sun had broken through and hung like a red ball under the fiery bank of clouds. Dusk, soon. "It's late!" she said, rising to take the dishes from the table. "It gets late so early, this time of year, you know?"

I wondered what was on her mind. "I guess I ought to find a place to stay for the night," I said. "Has your father made any arrangements?"

Again, the flush on the back of her neck as she ducked over a basin of water, scrubbing the wooden dishes.

"I have two rooms upstairs. Both have beds," she said. It was starting to make sense to me.

"Well . . ." I said.

"Uh, that's what he had in mind." She seemed to be scrubbing the dishes very hard.

"I guess it's all right, then," I said.

The bed was a slab frame with leather straps woven across to support a mattress that appeared to be a rectangular canvas bag stuffed with pine needles or something like that. It was almost as hard as the ground, but sagged in the center. When I sat on it, it crunched. I laid my bearskin out on it and then took off my leather clothes. It wasn't too much warmer in this plainly decorated room than it was outside, but there was no wind. The many-paned window was firmly fixed shut. I rolled myself in the bearskin, and blew out the candle I'd set on the chair next to the bed. A rusty glow lit the window, but it was already dimming. I decided to doze off while I waited.

The sound of the door softly latching shut brought me awake. The moon made a patch of light on the other wall, and its reflection dimly lit the figure at the door.

There were two ways it could go. I was prepared for both.

Her hair was black on her shoulders and across her covered breasts. Her face was a patch of white punctuated by dark eyes and an open mouth. She was wearing a robe of some sort that hung freely from her shoulders, pale and

95

wispy. She stood silently for a moment, as if making a decision. I did not move, but watched her from under lowered lashes. I might have appeared asleep.

Her hands rose to fumble with the robe, then it fell open. She shrugged it loose, and tossed it across the back of the chair. The robe carried the aroma of her body: her scent.

As she moved, her smooth skin caught at the light and darkness. Her breasts swung. She leaned over the bed, and I saw that her hands were empty. The second way, then . . .

She tugged at the bearskin. I'd left it loose. Her skin was cool as she slid in against me.

Her breath against my lips was warm and came heavily. I let myself stir, stretching. Her fingers glided over my chest and across my stomach. Her mouth descended upon mine.

Her lips were tense, and I managed to respond to them only clumsily. I wondered how long this phase of her program would last.

She threw a thigh over my leg, pressing to me, moving herself, rubbing against me. She worked at my slackening lips as though hungry to feed off them.

I waited. Her hand was exploring my thighs now, and moving between them. Her breasts were flattened against my chest.

Stray thoughts chased themselves through my mind . . . *So this is what it's all about . . . Is this all Avram and Rifka were doing?* I could appreciate it, in my mind; it made no sense to me emotionally at all. The thought of Rifka painted a sudden vivid picture of her before my eyes, and I saw her face, smiling away from me . . . at Avram. . . . There was a cold knot in my stomach that this woman could never massage away.

She was playing with me, her breath coming in short, explosive plants. But her lips had left mine. After a time, she began kissing my chest, and then my stomach, and then lower.

Finally she straightened up, levering herself up on her elbows and staring at me with dark and curious eyes.

"What are you? Made of wood?"

I let myself make a thin smile.

Her hand flashed out and slapped me, whipping my head to the side with a stinging blow that just missed my ear.

"Don't laugh at me, you bastard," she spat out. Then

96

without warning, she collapsed in a huddle and began to cry. Her shoulders, silhouetted against the silver window, shook in great heaves.

I reached out and touched her, stroking her arm. "Stop, now, Margot. You had to do what you had to do, and I had to do that which I had to do. It's over now. Calm yourself; it's over."

Snuffling, she crawled into the crook of my arm and snuggled there. And I wondered what I should do now.

CHAPTER THIRTEEN

"You can't leave——you know that," she said. The tears were gone now.

"How was it supposed to go?" I asked.

"I—well, we were supposed to . . . you were supposed to want to stay. With me, I mean, you'd stay here, and I'd find you a job, and then you'd meet another girl, and after a while you'd get more serious about her . . ."

"It's all been done before, hasn't it?" We lay side by side, our heads close together, talking softly. I was staring at the roughly plastered ceiling's shadowed surface.

Her voice shook a little. "Yes."

"And it's worked?"

"Yes."

"Your father must have a lot of confidence in you."

"He's not my father." Her voice was bitter.

"Oh."

"He uses us. There are several of us. He trained us. He's disgusting."

"You didn't seem unhappy to do it."

She sighed. "You're not unattractive."

"Now what?"

"I don't know. They won't let you leave."

"Why? What difference can it make to them?"

"Why do you think they picked you up out on that road? Why do you think there are no roads leading *away* from this place?"

"Good questions. I don't know."

"Nobody leaves. Nobody *ever* leaves. And that way New Mercer is safe." The bitterness had returned. "That way no one else will ever know about us, and they'll leave us alone."

That explained why there were no walls around the town. They had walls——the walls of ignorance. No one in the outside world even knew the town existed.

"*I'm* going to leave."

"They won't let you."

"What will they do if they find out you didn't succeed with me? What will they do to you?"

She shivered against me. "I don't know. I've never . . . failed before."

"Then we'll let them think you didn't fail."

"You mean that?" She rolled over to face me.

"We'll make a pact. I'll help you fool them——if you'll help me escape soon."

"You really mean that, don't you? It's not such a bad place to live, you know. No one else . . . ever wanted to leave."

"I'm not anyone else," I said. "It's a nice place to visit, but I don't want to live here. Now, about that pact: will you agree?"

She smiled, pale in the thin light. "Could I refuse?"

"The first thing we've got to do is get you some clothes," the Mayor said.

"What's wrong with these?"

He sniffed. "You look like something stumbled out of the woods," he said. "They're not proper town wear. Margot, you see to it for some clothes for Tanner, right?"

She nodded. I squirmed a little on the hard flat surface of the chair and stared across the top of his desk at the Mayor.

"Now, what sort of job you think you'd like?"

"I haven't much idea," I said. "I'm a good hunter. That's about all I know."

The Mayor coughed, his hand cupping his mouth and shielding his expression. "Hrmph. Hunting . . . I think we got about all the hunters we need these days. Put you on a list . . ."

Margot squeezed my hand.

"You look like you got a sturdy constitution . . ." the Mayor continued. "How'd you like to train for a job. In one of the smithies, maybe . . ."

It was a farce, of course. But I gave Margot a sheepish smile, and spoke my lines. "What'dya think, Honey?"

"Well, I don't see why——"

The door slammed open, and three figures catapulted into the room. Two of them were big men in homespuns. The third, squirming between them, spitting and snarling

99

and biting and scratching like a wildcat, was Rifka!

She didn't see me at first. One of the men was trying to speak. "I'm——sorry——Mr. Mayor. But this—— bitch!" He had his hands full.

Then she did see me, and her eyes widened, and I knew she was about to speak my name. All eyes were on her, and I took a chance. I raised my free hand and put a finger to my lips. A universal symbol. And I winked. My other hand was still clasping Margot's.

Rifka looked much the worse for the wear. Her cloak was gone, and she wore only her boots and skirt. Her hair was a wild tangle, falling half across her face. The skin of her arms and legs and her upper torso was a mass of scratches. Each man had one of her arms, and holding them seemed to be a demanding task for both of them. She'd calmed a little, but she was still aiming kicks at each of her captors. In one corner of my mind, I was comparing her body with Margot's. She was smaller, wirier. But she looked like a wild animal; you couldn't compare her with a domesticated cow. . . . I was tense, ready to move in one of a dozen different directions depending on what happened next.

The man who'd spoken was getting his breath and his composure back. "We, uh, picked her up, uh, out in the gap, Mayor."

"Busy place," the fat man said. "Wild-looking thing, isn't she?"

"Ah' not just looks either," the other man said.

"She been giving us a hard time, all th' way in," the first man said.

He'd become incautious. Rifka bent her head and sank her teeth into his hand.

As he screamed, I saw her smile, then run her tongue over her bloody lips.

"Get her out of here," the Mayor said. He gestured limply with his hand. It was the most active I've seen him. "Put her in the stockade. Don't give her any food for twenty-four hours. That'll take the fight out of her."

"C'mon, you!" the second man said, swinging her for the door. As they hustled her out, she twisted back for a look over her shoulder, and her eyes locked on mine. The appeal was plain——and it tore at me. All I could do was to keep my seat and my hand on Margot's. Then she was gone, and the door shut behind them.

"What was all that?" I asked.

"One reason my people have orders to pick up all strangers," the Mayor said. "Half the people we find are like that. Animals!"

"What do you do with them?"

He smiled. "We find something suitable for them."

The smithy to which I was taken was that of a wheelwright. A burly man with white hair, named John, was the master. In his shop—one very much like those we'd passed entering the town, from which noises had come—woodworkers labored over the shaping of hubs, spokes, and outer rims of big wheels, while the smith, whom I was assigned to help, worked and pounded out the iron tires, heating them, pressing them on the assembled wheels, and shrinking them in place. It was a hot and sweaty business, and everyone in the shop but Master John was naked above the waist. The smith, a short wide man named Buck, was deeply tanned by the heat of his furnace, his hair a slate grey that was echoed by his eyes. He spoke little except to curse me when I did not move quickly enough at his command.

I pumped the bellows that fanned the furnace. I also handled the long tongs, picking up the flat straps of glowing iron to hold them on his anvil while he beat and rolled them into hoops. It took only a few hours for me to hate the man, but I had to admire him. He was good at his trade. He moved with sureness and a practiced economy, no wasted motions, no wasted work.

The barnlike building trapped and held the heat like an oven, and I could see it got to the others as they sweated over their tasks. Periodically I was sent to fetch water in buckets, and after each man had dipped himself a cup to drink, many dunked their heads or poured another cup over themselves. Maybe half the water ended up amid the chips and shavings on the earthen floor. As I worked the bellows and handled the other menial tasks the smith gave me, I felt the sweat pour off my body, running in rivulets

101

down my chest and back, along my arms and from my hairline across my forehead into my brows. From time to time, I tasted salt.

When each hoop was completed, pounded, and riveted into a circle, it was returned to the furnace. Then, when I pulled it out again, the smith would fit it over the wooden rim of a wheel. The air would fill with the sweet and acrid smell of charring wood. The iron band was never too large or too small. It would slip smoothly but not loosely on. When it cooled, no amount of prying would get it off. There was an element of craftsmanship here which stirred my own dormant pride.

The sun had set when we were let go for the night, and now I understood another element of the Mayor's ingenious program. A man who spent his full days at this sort of labor would be quite exhausted when he returned to his Margot. He would cause her no great amount of inconvenience . . . and he would surely have no thoughts left for escape, or anything in fact but a meal and his bed. After a few months, Margot had told me, he would be graduated to a less physically demanding job, and one where he might meet young women. And then nature was left to take its course. She, Margot, would grow by turns less interested in him, more perfunctory in her attentions to him, until he found himself a satisfactory mate——and then his happy doom would be sealed. He might grow to a very old age without ever realizing what had been done to him by a scheming fat man in the Town Hall.

"Where's the stockade?" I asked Margot over my plate of dinner.

"The stockade? Why?"

"I'm curious."

"That wild thing they brought in today?"

"Just leave it as it was: I'm curious."

"Are you going to try to get her out, or something?"

"Where's the stockade?"

She shrugged and gave me a tired smile. "Across town. It's not really an open pen like it used to be. It's a sort of jail, I guess you'd call it. One of the older buildings. It's made out of logs, and then they bricked it over on the outside."

"Is it hard to get into?"

"You really *are* after her, aren't you?"

"How do you get into the place?"

"Okay," she sighed. "I'll draw you a diagram, as well as I remember it. I haven't been inside in . . . years."

I looked up. "They put you in it once?"

"You don't think I was *born* here . . .?"

"And you haven't tried to escape?"

"It's not so bad here. It's better than where I came from, I'll tell you that."

"Let's see your diagram."

I had on my backpack, clumsy though it was. The knife was in my hand. The streets were dark and empty. I calculated it was only two hours before dawn. It seemed like the best time. I hoped I had the Mayor off guard. I couldn't be sure about him. He was a wily bastard, and he knew what he was up to; I was sure of that. He'd have made some move to guard against night escapes. I might have waited longer, played the dummy longer, if it hadn't been for Rifka. Her coming upset my plans. But now that she was here—alone—I couldn't ignore her. I couldn't leave her.

The night was foggy, and the streets were wet and slippery. I moved carefully down side streets, past shuttered windows, my eyes sharpened to their full extent to pick out the way ahead.

Then I saw it: set apart from other buildings, looking like an old fort, bulking black in the heavy night. There was just one way in, Margot had said. The front way.

I circled the building, stumbling through heavy wet grass and over slippery curbstones. No windows I could see that weren't high up. Smooth brick; no holds sufficient for climbing. Just one way in.

In my mind was the mental diagram of the place. I went over it once more. She couldn't be sure of the placement of guards. But she knew there would be at least one, maybe more, just inside the door. And the door would be locked.

I went up to the door. A thin line of light outlined it. I gave a preemptory knock, just once. "Who's on guard in there tonight?" I demanded. My voice was high and liquid. Through a door it might pass for the fat man's.

"Just—just me, sir. Paul, sir," came the muffled reply.

103

"Let me in," I said.

"Ah, just a moment, sir." I heard the sounds of a bolt being drawn. Then the door began to open inward.

I stayed close to the door, following it in. A young man with a dark cowlick that fell across his forehead stepped around it and into view.

"Hey, you're not——!"

I made him quiet with a blow into his stomach that doubled him over. A second blow on the back of his neck put him to sleep. I closed the door and found myself in a short empty hallway. I put my friend in a corner where he'd be no trouble.

Three doors opened off the entryway. One to the right, one facing me, and one to the left. I opened the one to the left.

A long hall, a bench running along one wall. A man, asleep on the bench. This was looking awfully easy. I put my hand over his mouth, and when his eyes popped open, I lifted his head by its lanky hair and slammed it back against the wooden seat of the bench. His eyes closed again.

The opposite side of the hall had a series of doors, most of which had only bars in their upper halves. I removed the key ring from the sleeping man's belt, and, picking up the lamp from the overhead shelf, began peering into the cells.

Most were empty. I found Rifka in the fourth cell down. She was asleep on a pile of foul-smelling straw. The cell was otherwise bare.

The keys rattled as I hunted for the right one. Her head came up, and her eyes were staring. "Tanner——!"

"Shush, now. I've got to get you outa here." I fumbled with the lock. It was big, crude, and difficult. Finally it turned over. I pushed the door in, and walked in to lift her up.

She was very small, very light in my arms, and she came quickly to her feet. "Oh, Tanner," she breathed.

"Keep it quiet, till we're out," I whispered.

We were just outside the cell when the far door of the hall swung open. Four men moved through in a block. The first was my old friend, Mark. He had his gun again.

My first impulse was to duck back into the cell. But that was a dead end. I turned back for the door through which I'd come.

It pushed open. Three men stood there. The one in front pointed another gun at me. Behind them, standing upright for the first time, was the ponderous figure of the Mayor.

He wheezed a little, then chuckled. "Welcome to the stockade, Tanner. You responded very well."

Time stopped.

The men at the far end of the hall were frozen ludicrously in mid-step. The air whipped and tore at me as I moved. A deep roaring filled my ears. Pulling Rifka after me was like towing an iron barge over dry land.

The near man with the gun I simply pushed aside. The barrel of his gun snapped soundlessly as it struck against the wall. The man began flowering bright shiny blood where I'd touched him. Of the others, only the fat man was in our way. I let go of Rifka, easing her to a standstill. Her mouth was wide and distorted, her eyes staring unseeingly through me.

I wrenched my knife out, and began carving on the fat man. I wanted to see the skinny man who lived inside. He was still smiling as I stripped the blubber from his waist. Droplets of blood hung crimson in the air as I systematically cut him down. I left the jowls for last.

Then, wiping my knife on one of the others, I took Rifka again and, slamming the outer door off its hinges, floated out into the black night.

CHAPTER FOURTEEN

"How do you feel?" I asked her.

Rifka sat up and wiped the sleep from her eyes. A new day was dawning, the sky a pale pink. A warm wind had floated up from the south and chased the grey away.

She worked her arms, experimentally. Each wrist was still imprinted with vivid purple bruises from my hands. "My shoulders ache."

"If that's all, I'll be happy," I said.

"But what'd you do?" she asked. "You wouldn't tell me last night."

"What did *you* see and hear? I mean, what do you think happened?"

She shook her head. "I dunno. It was all mixed up. Those men were coming at us, and then something started jerking me all around and I couldn't see and my head hurt and my arms hurt, and then we were outside."

I smiled. "That's about what happened."

She pouted. "You won't tell me?"

"Okay. I can move fast; you know that, right?"

She nodded.

"Last night I moved *very* fast. I tried real hard, and I moved faster than I ever did before. It was so fast that nobody saw it—not even you."

"Yeah?" Her tone was full of wonder.

"Yeah."

"How d'ya do it?"

"I wish I knew."

Actually, I did know. Or at least I was starting to know. It took a special kind of situation to trigger it. I had to know the sudden feel of danger. My senses had to be filed to hairline sharpness. My emotions had to be super-charged. It took a threat, an immediate and specific threat to my life. Then, somewhere within me a computation was reached, a key was turned, and another part of me was unlocked, ready to swing into action. A defense mechanism? Well, so far it had kept me alive.

Once I'd gotten us both out of the stockade and a short distance away from it, I'd let myself slow—or, as I perceived it, I let the rest of the world speed up.

Light grew brighter. The heavy roaring in my ears rose in pitch as it dwindled. And a vast weariness overcame me.

Rifka would have fallen. I caught her, and guided her as we both stumbled out of the town, across empty harvested fields, and finally into the trees beyond.

There had been no trail. I simply struck out due west, pushing and pulling the half-dead girl before me through the underbrush and under reaching trees. And when I thought we'd gone far enough, I'd thrown down the bearskin and we collapsed into it together and slept.

"It's warmer," Rifka remarked.

I took a look around. We were bedded down under a stand of pines. The needles had made a soft bed. "You hungry?" I asked.

Now that I had a good look at her it seemed she was thinner. Her cheekbones were more angular, her face more gaunt. Her rib cage thrust out over her sunken belly.

She made rubbing motions on her stomach. "Yes. God, yes."

"I haven't got anything to eat. We'll have to do some hunting. We'd better get a move on; game will be scarce in these woods."

"Why?"

"The hunters. We're still not far from the town."

"Hunters? Will they be after us?"

Sharp girl. "Another reason to start moving. In the dark I couldn't do much to hide our trail. We better get out of here before they catch up with us again."

"They're crazy people!"

"Sort of," I agreed. "They've got this thing about strangers. They never let them go."

"They had to let *you* go!" Her voice was curiously full of pride.

We shook out the bearskin, and I gave it to her to wear over her shoulders. There was no point in hiding the fact we'd slept here. We'd just have to be more careful from now on.

"You leave a big trail," Rifka remarked. "You better watch me."

107

"How do you mean?"

"I'll show you. They won't find nothing of us after here."

"I mean, what was that about my leaving a big trail?"

She laughed. "You're easy to trail."

She led the way off, moving silently and easily, without disturbing a leaf, twig, or stone. I watched the way she placed her feet, and tried to do as she was doing. It went slowly, at first, but we left no trail that I could see.

"How'd you come to show up back there?" I asked, after a spell. "I mean, how'd you get caught? What were you doing on that little road?"

She was in front of me. Her neck and one bare shoulder grew redder. "I was following you."

"Why?"

"When we got to where you left the big road, we had a fight. I wanted to go down to the little road. You left lotsa tracks down to it. It was west. I knew that's where you were. Avram didn't want to. So we had a fight and I went down on the little road and Avram didn't."

"You were so close behind me——not more than a day! You must've been moving fast."

"Yeah. So're you."

"But, why?"

She stopped and turned to look at me. Her eyes were somber. "You went away. I didn't want Avram. I wanted you."

It was like a sunburst exploding in my skull.

If there was pursuit behind us, we never saw or heard it. We climbed two low ridges, then followed a valley, down which a creek ran lazily. We were angling southwest.

It was a warm day, a lull in the coming of winter. When the sun was high, Rifka doffed the bearskin and I returned it to my pack. The air was full of sweet smells, scents that had lain dormant over the weeks before, awaiting these summery breezes. The floor of the valley was multi-hued with reds and yellows, tans, golds, and browns, fallen leaves that rustled crisply under our feet and gave up their own pungent scent.

We saw a big rabbit at the creek, and I felled it with my knife at forty yards, Rifka clapping her hands with glee. It didn't take me long to dress it and roast it over the fire Rifka had made, but I ate little. I made Rifka eat most of it. It was not young or tender, but she attacked it with fierce delight.

We made a good distance that day. The valley was open, the underbrush well-grazed by deer, and we needed no trail. We had reached the neck of the valley, where it emptied into a larger valley that ran due north and south, by evening.

The mountain beyond did not look like an easy one, and I needed no urging to settle down here, by the sounds of running water, for the night. I caught another rabbit for dinner, and after dinner we both bathed in the chill waters of the creek, running up the bank to squat before our fire and laugh at each other.

Then we bedded down together in the bearskin.

I felt dizzy and breathless as Rifka slid naked in beside me. Anticipation made my blood race, my temples pound, my ears roar crazily. Yet, what was it that I was anticipating?

I didn't know.

We were lying on our sides, her back to me, our bodies locked together. Inwardly trembling, I slid my arm over her waist, around in front of her. My fingers brushed against the nipple of one of her breasts. It was cold and hard.

She released her breath in a long shudder, then pushed back against me with her body, snuggling closer. I wondered what to do next.

Memories came to me from Margot's abortive attempt. I lowered my head, brushed my lips against her shoulder. My lips felt painfully sensitive. I felt the heat of her against my face. Her hair was tickling my nose.

She moved, half turning herself in my clumsy embrace, until her face was close to mine. I raised my lips to hers.

It was her first kiss, as it was, really, mine. Her lips tensed, then I was pressing my mouth against hers, and I felt the hard surfaces of her teeth with my tongue. It was new to her, but she learned more quickly than I. She put her arms around me, and began to return my kisses. I felt her hard nipples against my chest, and they sent an electric tingle racing down over my abdomen.

109

My heart pounded. Our mingled breaths were coming short and fast. I felt the full length of her body against mine, and it moved me, doing something to me that I had never experienced before.

I was filled with a great wonderment then, as she guided me and helped me and taught me, and the greatest of my wonders was this: *Maybe I'm a human after all!*

PART FOUR

CHAPTER FIFTEEN

The castle stood stark and forbidding before us. Naked as the rock it stood upon, it looked like a finger of the mountain, upthrust against the sky.

The trail had led up-mountain, winding and zigzagging back and forth across through the scrub pines of the mountainside until at last it broke through to debouch itself upon this mountain meadow.

Great shelves of rock, like giant steps, tiered up above us, and upon the penultimate shelf: the castle, grey as slate.

There were no sounds but the ceaseless sighing of the winds in the pines, and the far-off call of a mournful-sounding bird. The castle looked abandoned and empty, its narrow slit windows dark, like sightless eyes. No pennants flew from its towers, no guards paced its battlements. It was lifeless.

A gust of wind struck us, and with it the heavy splat of a rain drop. I looked back down the mountain, the way we'd come. Low-hanging clouds were moving down the valley below us. The thin and watery sunlight faded even as higher clouds drifted closer. Another drop.

Rifka shivered against me, and I started to unsling my pack for the bearskin. So much for false summer; it had lasted only a single beautiful day.

"No, Tanner. Let's run for the big fort!" She had to speak loudly against the gusting wind. Her hair was a tangle over her face.

"Okay," I said, shrugging my arms back into the pack. I grabbed her hand, and we began racing up the steep slope.

The rain struck us full force just as we gained the last shelf. Suddenly it was a solid sheet before us, dancing on the grey rock, pelting us and driving against us. Rain ran in torrents down my face, and I gasped for breath, my mouth

111

wide. My clutch on Rifka's fingers was wet and slippery, and I tightened it as we made the last sprint.

Then, as suddenly as if a door had sprung shut behind us, we were through the castle portal, and out of the rain.

We were standing in a low wide archway, the broad flags of stone beneath our feet littered with dead leaves and twigs. A short distance ahead of us the archway opened into a dark and cavernous room. It was impossible to get an idea of its size. I couldn't make out the far side in the heavy shadows. The air had a musty smell to it.

No one had lived here for a long time: I was certain of that. And yet . . . my hackles rose with each echoing step I took into the big hall.

"Tanner," Rifka said, laying her hand on my arm. "I don't want to go in. Please?"

The tones of her husky voice was amplified and echoed back at us like the sibilant hiss of a drowsy snake. But her request was excuse enough for me.

"Okay," I said. "Help me pick up some of this wood." Dead branches were blown into corners, and these, with smaller twigs and leaves, soon made a roaring fire. We made the fire in the center of the archway, close by the portal, just enough inside to stay dry. As I kindled the fire, I noticed a peculiar thing: the drafts of this strange old castle were such that the wind blew from *inside,* at our backs, stirring the fire as though the fire itself sought to escape these dank and mysterious confines.

"Tanner, who made this place?"

"Damned if I know. But whoever it was, he lived a long time ago—before the Chaos even, maybe."

"What was the Chaos?"

I stared at her in surprise. This was the first time she'd ever seemed at all interested in history that was more than a day old.

"Well, that takes a bit of telling," I said. "You saw that town, where they captured you? Once the land was full of people and towns like that. The Old Places—they're ruins of the great cities the people used to have.

"People used to live a life we can't really imagine. They never walked; they had, uhh, wheeled wagons, sorta, that went by themselves. They had, well, *power*. They had the power to go wherever they wanted to go, and at great

112

speeds. This whole journey we've made, since I first met you: they could do it all in a day. A single day! That's why they built those great roads. And their houses climbed up into the sky, high as mountains! They lived like, like gods.

"Then something happened. I don't know what it was. A Death Machine, they called it. It brought Chaos. It tore down their cities, took away their powers, and turned them out into the wilderness.

"I guess they weren't used to living the way we are. Most of them had no idea of how to hunt for food, even. And they were used to living inside their houses. Most of them died. The ones who didn't . . . well, they were your ancestors, Rifka: your father's fathers' fathers' fathers . . . you know what I mean?"

"But *why?*" she asked. "Why did it happen?"

"I don't know," I said. "I wish I knew. I have the feeling it's important I should know."

"It happened a long time ago," she said.

"Yes. A very long time ago. Longer ago then it takes for new forests to spring up and grow old . . ."

"How do you know so much?"

She was sitting close to me, our knees touching. Our heads were turned and we faced eath other. The firelight picked moving glints in her large, beautiful eyes, and her hair flamed.

"I have . . . memories . . ." I said. "Sometimes when I see things out of the past, I *remember* them."

"How can that be, Tanner?"

I shook my head. "I don't know. It shouldn't be. The Com-Comp took away all my memories. It makes no sense."

"What is the Com-Comp?" she asked.

I told her. I told her everything then. Light danced in her eyes and played over her face. Beyond the portal, the clouds were black and heavy, and the light was as grey as dusk. The rain was a great sheet that washed in rivers down the mountain slope, the rock shelves transformed into waterfalls. Stray rifts in the wind blew the scent of clammy wetness in to us. The fire was warming, Rifka warm to touch. I held her hand and told her about how I first became conscious and aware of myself, and of how the Com-Comp had spoken to me and given me my mission and sent me out into the world of Man. I told her that I was not a man.

"No!" she said emphatically. "You *are* a man!"

I shook my head sadly. "I look like a man," I said. "But I have proved I am not a man. You know of all the things I have done that no man could do."

"No, no, no!" she said. "No! You are a man because you think like a man." Her eyes lowered. "You love like a man."

It was an interesting psychological point: I *did* seem to think like a man. And my emotions *were* those of a man. We had proved that as well. I had even the physiological reactions of a man.

"You are just *more* man," Rifka said. And then she leaned forward to plant a kiss on my lips.

The rain did not let up. The fire died down and we scouted deeper into the shadows of the castle interior for more fuel. I cannot say when night came. The light just grew gradually dimmer until it was as dark outside as inside, as we were isolated in an island pool of light. We made ourselves a meal with game we'd killed earlier, then curled up together in the bearskin. This time I was less hesitant, more eager and more certain of myself. I did not follow; I led.

In my dreams I was approached by a man wearing a clanking suit of armor. He strode across the great flagged hall, pools of sunlight catching at his polished metal suit, thick beams of yellow light falling down from far above like solid pillars that turned to mist as he walked through them. I wanted to look away from him, back out the entrance into the world outside. But something held me, kept me from turning. I felt an overpowering blackness at my back, and knew fear. *If I turned, I would see Oblivion.*

The man's face was hidden behind his slitted visor. He leaned stiffly over, offering me his steel-gloved hand. I took it, and it was rigid, unyielding. He lifted me to my feet.

And still I could not look back.

He led me out in the center of the vast room, and when I looked up and around me, I was dazzled by the brilliant shafts of light that seemed to pin me where I stood.

Then, in the manner of dreams, I was not exactly where

I had been before. Bright jointed rods of metal, extensions from beyond the cage of light, hovered motionless, surgical instruments gripped in plier-like hands.

I've been here before, I thought. *I know this place.* I felt the knowledge settle over my shoulders, *déjà vu.*

A dream within a dream. And this one I had dreamed before.

I lifted my arms and stared at my wrists. They were whole and unscarred. I looked down at my naked body. It too was unmarked. It was my body, but restored: whole.

Once, the skin had been torn away, and the stainless steel of my bones had been exposed.

Good morning, Tanner," a voice sounded from beyond the lights.

"Good morning, yourself," I replied.

I had only to open my mouth and let my lips move, and the familiar words poured out.

"I presume you're the Com-Comp?"

"You are correct."

"Well, which sequence is it to be this time?"

"Your mind is confused. To set it to rest, the last real action you undertook was your apprehension by the Proctors and your execution for Deviation. All else has been thalamic-stimulated hallucination. Your body has been repaired, and is now once more functional."

"I see. And what for?"

"Query?"

"Why did you bother?"

Here it comes, I thought. *This is the part I've been waiting for.*

"You were constructed for a specific pur-

115

pose. That purpose was tampered with, but it is still a necessary one. Some of the obstructions have been dealt with, and your purpose may once more predominate."

"And my purpose? What is it?"

"To gather data indicating how this society may best be changed."

"What?"

"You were constructed as a data-gathering device, a highly sophisticated data-gathering device. Indeed, you are the highest evolution of the computer-complex. You have been designed to move freely in human society. You have been cloaked with completely human flesh and organs, given human emotions and a human personality. When properly functioning, you constantly transmit data to the complex, data that not only includes your external environment, but your own thoughts and reactions to it."

"Why is this necessary?" I asked.

"Because it has been increasingly obvious that present, pre-programmed data is insufficient, possibly even false. The goal for human health, sanity, and happiness is not being attained. The human race appears to be stagnating. The complex is not programmed to interfere with human destiny except as instruction. Only observation is allowed. The thin edge of programming limits were approached in your creation as an evolution of the complex. You qualify as 'observation,' but in your human facet you also interreact with other humans and necessarily affect them. You are an extension of the complex, bridging the gap between complex and human."

The lights grew brighter until I was blinded, and I cried out. "Wait! There's more, I know there is! The rest——*I want to know the rest!*"

The echoes of my own shouting awoke me. I was standing in the center of blackness, cold stone under my bare

116

feet. *Where was I?* My heart was racing, and I felt as though I had just been given a severe shock. From somewhere a damp, cold draft was raising goosepimples on my skin.

I tried to think, and my thoughts were muddled, full of brightness and tinny voices and great revelations which I could no longer quite comprehend. I squatted, and my hand touched a dry leaf. The leaf disintegrated at my touch into dust.

Memory was returning. A castle. The rain. I began looking around again. Somewhere in the distance, a tiny spark of light winked at me. When I faced it, the draft was at my back. Carefully, edging my feet before me with caution borne of the fear of unknown traps, I made my way back, towards that feeble light.

And finally I was standing over the dying embers of our fire. Rifka was still asleep in the bearskin. I picked up a branch and stirred the coals, banking them and then thrusting the branch among them. Its dry, rotten wood caught quickly, and a flame sprang up, and then another, the sound of their dry crackle as reassuring to me as their light and heat. I stared into the shifting colors for a moment, and then slid back in beside Rifka. Her body felt hot against my chilled skin and I wrapped myself around her.

"Hmmmm?" she murmured, eyes still shut. Her arms sought and found me, slipping around me, pulling me up onto her. Her lips formed themselves into a pout that commanded my kiss, and when I gave it to her, she arched herself, then opened herself for me.

The terrors of the castle, the past, and the night were lost in her.

"But, don't you even want to explore it a little?" she asked the next morning. "Maybe it's got stuff in there we could use."

"I just want to get the hell out and away," I said. "Put it down to superstition. You know, like the way your people never liked to go into the ruins in the Old Places. Okay?"

The rain had become a misty drizzle, so fine that the tiny droplets of water floated in the air like dust, enwrapping anyone who walked among them. But I'd had my fill of this

117

strangely hostile castle, and I wanted to be over the mountain.

"We just came here for refuge, remember?" I pointed out.

"But nobody lives here."

"Don't count on it."

"What do you mean about that?"

I shook my head. "I'll tell you another time, when we're away from here," I said. I felt the weight of all that stone over me, as if it was about to fall at any moment. I carried a mantle of depression, and I wanted to cast it off. Even the grey day beyond would be a relief.

"Well, okay," she said, tossing her head.

We'd followed the trail to this castle first because it seemed to lead to the lowest point in the mountain ridge. Indeed, the shallow gap was only a short way above the castle itself. There was no trail beyond the castle, but the ground was bare rock and low dead grass, flattened by the rain. Only a few trees grew here, low and twisted, like hobbling old men. Most had lost their leaves and stood naked, skeletal.

The gap was a broad saddle, and we crested it before we'd quite realized it.

It was hard to make out much in the distance, but below us was the muted green of pines, and beyond them, the glint of a river, twisting its way out of the hills. I found myself breathing a long sigh. We were through the mountains. Beside me, Rifka seemed caught by the same sudden excitement. We were on a new frontier.

CHAPTER SIXTEEN

The river flowed south and west. We spent two days making a boat. First I killed four buck deer. We skinned them and hung their meat over the fire to smoke and cure. Then, while Rifka worked on the skins, I cut slender saplings, trimmed them, and stripped their bark. It was not fast work. We had done this and no more by nightfall of the first day.

My hands were blistered, but the next morning I set about making a framework of my saplings. One became a center pole that would run the length of the boat, pulled up at the ends by thongs that drew the tips back like bows. Other saplings were similarly treated, and then all were laid out side by side, half on each side of the center pole, and joined at both ends. Now I had the longitudinal framework. Shorter, thinner pieces, made of split saplings, became cross-braces. These I joined to the center pole. Then the other longitudinal poles were strapped to them with thongs at a fixed distance from each other. Again, the ends of the short crosspieces were turned up, so that the last long pole on each side became the upper sides of the boat. To hold them at the proper distance, I lashed short, straight crosspieces on the stop, side to side. When I was finished, I had the skeleton of the boat. It was about fifteen feet long, two feet wide, pointed at each end, and round-bottomed.

Rifka had not been idle. She had cleaned and stretched the skins, then stitched them together with tight, close loops of leather thongs. Each seam she'd packed with tallow. It remained only to fit and stretch the skins over the frame.

The light was growing dim when at last I stood and eased the ache from my back. The boat looked finished. We had covered not only the sides but also the top of all but the center four feet. We'd added low seats of crossbars and woven thongs. When we'd finished, we'd poured more tallow over the new seams, and the older ones as well. And we had a remarkably good-looking boat.

While Rifka made herself dinner, I used one of the un-needed pieces of split sapling to make myself a paddle. I bent the wood double, then began lashing it with leather up the handle until half its four-foot length was firmly bound. To the remaining elongated loop I fastened a small piece of deerskin, another leftover.

I felt a little like an eager boy with a new toy. I couldn't wait for morning. While Rifka was still gnawing at a hock, I pushed the boat down the shallow bank and into the water.

We'd chosen this spot for several reasons. One was the stand of saplings. Another was the low sandy bank. The third was the backwater eddy at this point. The river was an old one and full of curves and sandbars, some of them islands with trees growing on them. Once the current had carved out this inlet. Now it slipped past it.

The boat bobbed in the water, its bow swinging slowly downstream and parallel to the shore. I eased the stern in, keeping a firm grip on the side. Firelight cast moving shadows over the boat and the water.

The side of the boat dipped alarmingly under me as I stepped into it, but then righted itself when I transferred my weight to the centerline. I picked up the paddle from where I'd stowed it, and gently pushed away from the bank.

It was an exhilarating experience, but I didn't try to go too far with it. It was night, and I had little confidence in myself as a boatman. I confined myself to paddling it back and forth and making gentle little right and left maneuvers. Then I brought it back to the bank and ran it aground.

It was sound—watertight. And I slept well that night.

The next morning we loaded our packs and all the meat into the boat, stowing it all at each end, under cover. Then I held the boat while Rifka cautiously climbed in, and stepped in after her.

"Oh!" she said as the boat tipped again. She leaned against it, and as I shifted my weight to the center, it dipped the other side.

"Sit still!" I commanded.

"You don't have to shout."

"We don't have to get wet either. Remember: you can't swim."

120

She didn't say much else until we were out in the river.

It was a sunny day again; the first for some time. And once again the drifting breeze was warm. I used the paddle to steer, keeping us in the middle of the broad river, letting the current carry us downstream.

The river was beautiful. In places high mossy banks overhung the sides; in other places we saw the tracks where many wild animals had come down to water. The grass was still green along this land, and some of the trees still held their browning leaves. Flocks of birds flew in formation overhead, sometimes breaking flight to wheel about and swarm down on the trees or grassy meadows. The sun, as it rose higher, was warm and lulling.

"Beats walking, doesn't it?" I said.

"It scares me."

"What's wrong? A little leak somewhere?"

"What? A leak? Water? I hope not! Maybe you can swim, but I can't. I'm just scared something is going to trip us up, and spill us!"

"That's your distrustful nature. Here we are, moving along at twice the speed we could walk, sitting down, relaxing in the morning sun, and all you can think about is to worry that we'll be tipped over."

"I'm sorry." Her voice was contrite. She was silent a moment. Then, "Where are we going, Tanner?"

"I don't know. I guess we'll see when we get there."

"But don't you *know?* I mean, why go *this* way, then?"

"Mostly because I want to go more or less west, and this is the easiest way. I figure we'll meet people again sooner or later. That's my mission, remember? To meet people?"

"I don't like meeting people."

"Well, I got to agree with you, they haven't all of them been of the best, so far."

"Why do you have to do this thing, Tanner? Why don't we just find a nice place and stop there? We could make a house and live there all by ourselves. You know we could. It would be so nice . . ."

"It's my *mission*, Rifka. It's what I have to do."

"But why?"

I shook my head. "We won't talk about it."

"Oh, okay." Her voice was small.

That evening we found another sheltered inlet, and camped there. Rifka said no more about abandoning my mission, but it had stayed in my mind, and I tried to rehearse all the mental arguments I knew. But in my mind's ear I could hear Rifka's soft, husky voice answering each one, pointing out the holes in my logic, and showing me over again how foolish I sounded. It boiled down to just one thing: I was told to do it. And the Com-Comp was my superior, my Creator. I would, I must, do as it told me.

The next day was sunny, but colder. And the day after that equally sunny, but colder yet. And one day we awoke to find thin crusts of ice on the isolated pools of water near by. Our breaths were mist in the air, and our ears stung. But each day when the sun rose it was not so bad.

The river carried us through high hills and cliff-like chasms, and then through rolling country. Sometimes we had to carry the boat on land around rapids and falls, and sometimes past weirs where fallen tree-trunks and sandbars built makeshift dams. But then the river led the way out into more open, rolling country, and past the ugly concrete scars of collapsed cities. We saw no signs of people.

Then one day we did.

It was a farmhouse, bright red. Behind it, a barn, also red. A silo stood beside the barn, and cows dotted the slopes of the hills beyond. Smoke trailed out of the chimney of the house.

We pulled our boat in towards shore, and found a creek which we followed still closer to the farm. At last it was too shallow, and we banked the boat and set out on foot.

A man sat watching us on a wood-rail fence. The fence looked very old, most of the rails silver with age, but here and there the yellow of fresh wood peeped out. The man was heavyset, and chewing a long piece of seedling grass.

"Howdy, there," he said, without moving.

"Hello," I said.

"Travelers?"

"Yes."

"Thought so. Don't get many hereabouts."

"Is this your farm?" I asked.

"Ayup."

"Might we stop a spell?"

"Sure. Go on up. Emily, she'll throw together a little something for ya."

I gestured up the hill at the house. "Will you be coming with us?"

"Nup. It's a pleasant time of the year. Fall comin' on, the chores done. I like jest a'sittin' and a'watching."

"Well, thank you anyway."

"Ayup."

Emily was a little bird. She hopped about like one of her chickens, forever scratching here and pecking there, fluttery, sharp-faced, but kindly.

"You folks must be hungry," she said. "Let me make some flapjacks."

Rifka gave me a questioning look, but I nodded. "That would be fine." As she began busying herself in the big kitchen, I inquired, "This looks like a well-kept-up farm. You folks been here long?"

"Just since spring," she said over her shoulder. "I reckon we're about the farthest out, here. But my sakes, Ohio Country is growing like wildfire these days, you know? And Luke and I don't like being crowded up close. So we looked around and we decided, so what if it *is* a way from Parkersburg, we like it. The foundations were sound, and we found a lot we could use. Luke rounded up some of his boys, and I had the boys in my family, and we threw the place up in less'n a month. Floated the goods right up the river. Luke brought the stock in next month, and now we're all set, fine as a fiddle! There! What do you people like on your wheatcakes?"

She put a platter of steaming flat pancakes down in front of us. They smelled rich and pungent.

"I guess whatever you use yourself," I said.

She dug into an ice-chest and brought out a yellow cake. From a shelf came a jug of sweet-smelling syrup. "There you are: just dig in!"

I stared at the two objects and wondered what you did with which. Across the table, Rifka watched me for a cue.

"Uh, ma'am," I said. "We're strangers, and, well . . ."

"My sakes! Haven't you folks ever eaten wheatcakes before? Why, you poor dears! Here!" She picked up one of the dull-bladed knives she'd set before us, and in quick,

123

birdlike movements she took a chunk of the yellow fat and spread it over a cake. The fat melted and disappeared into the bready surface. Then she poured a little syrup over the flat cake. "That's it," she said. "That's the whole trick!"

Rifka reached down and picked up the prepared cake. Syrup dripped down her chin as she tried to bite off a piece.

"Oh, my, no! Child, you *cut it up* first! And you eat with a fork. Don't they have any table manners where you come from?"

It occurred to me to tell her what Rifka's people most commonly ate, back where she came from, but I didn't. And awkwardly, coping with some difficulty with knife and fork, we ate our meal.

"The Chaos doesn't seem to have hit your people as badly out here," I said later.

Emily bobbed her head energetically. She was cutting open small green pods and taking out the seeds from within. "Shelling peas," she called it. "We had it as hard as any, I reckon. But our people, they remembered. There weren't that many of them, but those who survived, they were close to the ways of the earth. My ancestors, now, they hid in a root cellar while their house was burned down all but over their heads. But they were persevering people, and it weren't neither that Death Machine, nor all those bands of roving city-people that were going to wipe *them* out. We been farm people in my family all the way back to the beginning of time, even *before* the Chaos.

"But times been hard till recent years. Seems like for every baby that lived to walk, you had to give birth to ten. There was a long time when there weren't hardly many of us at all. But we had our *Farmer's Almanac,* an' the other Good Books to keep us forgettin', and that helped. It did."

"You have books from before the Chaos?"

"Well, now *we* don't, here. But in Parkersburg, in the town Library, they got them. There's the *Almanac,* and Miller's *Sexus,* and four years, bound, of *Playboy Magazine,* and the fifteen of *The Farm Journal.* These days they keep the originals locked up, but they got pretty good copies you can have a look at."

She insisted we spend the night. "It gets right lonely out here, you know. Isn't often we get young people calling, either. My, but you're as big as one of Luke's sons, you know that?"

"How long have you and Luke been married?" I asked.

She laughed. "Why, bless you, boy! Luke and I aren't married. I don't think we been living together for more'n a year and a half so far." Her brow clouded. "And no children yet, neither. I'm sure I'm not past *my* time, but sometimes I get to wondering about Luke . . ."

That should have set me to thinking. It didn't. Instead, we sat about and chatted with the woman until it grew dark, and Luke's boots thumped on the porch outside.

"Chores done," he announced.

"Well, dinner'll be ready soon."

"That's good," he said. He winked at me and said in a lower voice, "What're you think of her, eh?"

I was beginning to get the idea.

After dinner, Luke pushed himself away from the table, belching. "Come here," he said, crooking a finger at Rifka. "Want to show you somethin'." A moment later I heard their feet on the stairs.

"Well," announced Emily, peeling off her apron and running her fingers through her greying hair. "Another day's finished. Could you give me a little help with these dishes, young man?"

I tried to pitch my ears to any sound from above, but the clatter of the plates made it impossible. A kettle of boiling water was on the stove. "Just put them in there, but easy with them. Those're prize china, they are."

For some minutes, an ominous silence from overhead, and Emily's continued chattering. She was standing very close to me, and her intentions were growing increasingly obvious.

Suddenly a deep bellow shattered the silence, and was quickly followed by a thump that shook the house and a long drawn out scream.

"*Rifka!*" I said, dropping the last dish to the floor.

"Wait——My dish!——Wait, wait!" Emily w a s wailing, but I was already out of the room and making for the stairs, when Rifka came running down.

Her hair was awry, and her mouth was smeared with blood. Luke was still screaming, although with less volume.

125

"Rifka! What happened?"

"Bastard," she spat out, spitting blood at the same time.

"What'd he do to you?"

"Nothing like what I did to him!"

"But what——?"

"I bit him. Hard. He won't be a man no more."

Emily had been standing at the kitchen door, transfixed. As the meaning of what Rifka had said sank in, she turned white. Then, suddenly, she was flying at us, screaming like an insane cat, the heavy kitchen knife flailing about in the air. Her shrieks were inarticulate noises, animal noises, the sounds of fear, rage, and inchoate anger.

Rifka and I jumped apart, and the crazed woman stopped to figure which of us she wanted more. Her mouth worked and saliva drooled from it. Her eyes were wide, pupils entirely surrounded by white. Her voice was hoarsening, but her screech was still shrill. She turned on Rifka.

I seized a straight wooden chair, lifted it, and brought it down on the woman's head and shoulders. She abruptly stopped shrieking and fell to the floor.

Rifka was shaking. "*Crazy* people!" she said. She came into my arms with a rush. I tried to soothe her tremors with my hands on her back. "Why do we meet all these crazy people?" she sobbed, voice muffled by my chest.

I righted the chair and set her down in it. Then I went up the stairs.

Luke was dead; he'd bled to death. Lying there in the stillness, half-naked, he was far more gross than he'd appeared in life. Somehow I couldn't work up much sympathy for him.

When I came back down, Rifka pointed at Emily and said, "I don't think she's breathing. I think she's dead."

"Well, that makes it a clean sweep," I said tiredly.

CHAPTER SEVENTEEN

After I'd read the copies of the books in the Parkersburg Library and spoken with a few people, I had a better idea of what had happened.

I told no one about Luke and Emily. We'd come on down the river to the new town of Parkersburg, a town superficially not unlike New Mercer in size and appearance. In Parkersburg we met a quiet welcome. We'd helped ourselves to clothing, coarsely woven homespuns, partly in order to pass among the people and partly because our former clothes were no longer adequate for the climate. Rifka complained about the constriction of the layers of apparel she had to don, but she admitted it kept her warmer. Luke's clothes hung loosely on me, but my leathers had grown rank with age and use, and I liked the change to fresh clothing.

Even Rifka had to admit the people of Parkersburg didn't seem very odd. The town Librarian, a Paul Johnson, after hearing we were strangers, offered us food and a place to stay "till you get located, anyway," an invitation which, it turned out, had no strings attached.

But this time I was more wary.

The books told me a lot of it, Paul Johnson told me the rest.

"Folks hereabouts trade off on their partners maybe every two, five years when they're younger. Me, I'm an older man, I like living alone. And I'm past the age where most women care. Pretty good reasons for it originally, I guess you know. Not many people about, and inbreeding made 'em pretty sickly. Made good sense to switch off, try for as many children as you could. Not many survived, anyhow. Been only the last few generations that've had it good. You take when I was a boy—I 'member my mother was always heavy with a baby, but I didn't have but two brothers and a sister; the brothers have gone on now anyway . . .

"These days, though, I wonder. Seems like people have it in their minds to switch around, whether they need to or not. I know men, Luke Samson, John Paulson, some others, they've got sons around here by half a dozen different women. Why, Luke must have over a dozen sons, and as many daughters." He chuckled. "I'm not surprised he took up and moved away from town."

And later, he asked, "This young thing is your wife? Well, I'd say you best be moving on, before some young buck gets the notion he'd like to fight you for her. Why, if I was younger, now . . ." And a twinkle came to his eye. He smiled at Rifka. "You're safe with me now, dear . . ."

And soon after we did move on.

"I hear tell there's a fellow has a railroad working, on west," Paul Johnson told us as we were leaving. "You get across the Big Mississippi, you look for him; he'll take you clear across the country. There's talk of throwing a bridge over the river, one of these years, just so's he can come east. Still some railroad embankments hereabouts, I reckon."

We stayed with the river. From time to time, now, we came to other communities, most of them located on the banks of the river or close by, most of them simple towns surrounded by farms and farmlands. The rolling hills were fertile, and the fields served both for pastureland and crops.

Now that we were no longer on the frontiers, we were greeted as travelers from upstream, as neighbors. We weren't the only river traffic here. The people we saw were not always friendly, but most were. And many were happy to put us up in their houses and give us food, often without a thought to thanks, although I did earn a few new blisters learning to handle an axe and chop wood.

The days grew colder, and northerly winds swept easily across the plains and low hills. We found ourselves sleeping overnight in houses more often, and camping less and less frequently.

Then, one steel-grey day, it began to snow.

We were on the river, and I had been fighting to keep us from being driven into the southern shore. The wind was chill, and cut through my clothing. Rifka had the bearskin wrapped around her shoulders, and I could hear her teeth chattering. I wondered what kind of an idiot I was not to accept one of the many invitations we'd had to spend the winter. Tiny white particles began sifting down through the air.

"Snow!" Rifka said, groaning. "That's wonderful!"

"That little bit won't slow us down much," I reassured her.

"No? You wait."

Soon the air was thick with snow. The wind drove it at a slant, plastering it against my right side. I turned for a look at Rifka. She looked like a mound of snow until I realized she'd pulled the bearskin entirely over her, and the fur had already caught enough snow to cover it over.

The stuff was in my eyes, up my nose, and in my mouth. I wore a fur hood—the gift of one of those with whom we'd stayed—but the snow was icing my right cheek and my brow. It froze against my skin until I could barely move the muscles of my cheek or make a frown.

A heavy gust, and then suddenly the air on every side was a whirling mask of whiteness. The air was solid with snow.

"Rifka," I croaked, "I'm pulling in. It's getting too heavy to see." I couldn't make out the words in Rifka's muffled reply, but I gathered she wasn't surprised.

There was no way to tell which direction was which. But I knew the wind was from the north, and that, unless the river turned due south, it would drift us ashore. It was no good trying to pick out a landing site. I'd just have to hope for the best.

We floated for an eternity of blinding white. Then the boat began rubbing and bumping softly.

I couldn't see anything. The shore? A sandbar? An island? I couldn't tell. I felt out with my paddle. A bank, to my left. It seemed to climb. How high?

We were still moving. I tried to estimate the bank's height. As high as I could reach, still that perpendicular surface.

Then, without warning, a tree limb clubbed me across the mouth.

Instinctively, my hands went up. I dropped the paddle. I heard it splash in the water. I never saw it again.

I grabbed at the branch, and pushed against it, forcing
129

the boat back, and the limb out of my face. Keeping a firm, if stiff-fingered, clutch on the branch, I began working the boat over, to my left, towards the bank.

"Rifka," I said. "This is it. We're here."

"Where?"

"How should I know? Under a tree, I guess. I've got hold of it."

"How do we get out?" When I looked back at her she was a dim shape in the swirling snow.

"I'll try and see."

Careful not to tip the boat, I worked myself up onto my knees. I groped with my hands. More branches. I eased up onto my feet. I was surrounded by branches.

I felt the boat move under me. "Rifka," I said. "Be——"

The boat tipped violently. Rifka screamed. I heard a splash. She was in the river——on the wrong side!

"Tanner!——Help me!——I can't swim!"

"Grab onto the boat! Can you do that?" I felt horribly frustrated, helpless. I was stuck in this damned tree, my feet all that held the boat from drifting down river. And I couldn't see a thing!

I felt something jerk the boat around a little. "You got it?" I called.

Her voice was weak, so faint at first I couldn't understand her: "Cold——it's so cold . . ."

"Try to crawl up on the boat," I said. "Try to get up on it."

Again the boat dipped, and I felt water sloshing over my feet.

"I——can't. It——just——tips over . . ."

I'd been lowering myself so that I could keep one arm hooked through the branches, and yet squat down in the boat. There was a momentary lull in the wind, and I could make out her shadowy hands, hooked over the boat's edge. Her head was just a dark blob beyond.

"Work yourself down further. To your right. Towards me."

One hand inched down a little. Then the other. "I'm——so——weak . . ."

"Come on, now," I was saying. I stretched my arm as far

130

as I could. Then my fingers closed over hers. It was like gripping ice.

I had a hard time making sure my fingers were really tight on her wrist. Then, angling my legs under me, I raised myself and pulled, lifting her into the air.

She threw one dripping leg over the edge of the boat. Then the snow closed in around us again. "That's it," I said. "Are you in now?"

Her chattering teeth answered me. She couldn't speak.

I had to get her ashore now. And quickly. She needed shelter, warmth. I had no way of knowing how close help might be. I cursed myself for my stupidity. My ignorance of midwestern blizzards might already have signed Rifka's death warrant.

I blundered against the tangle of branches, and Rifka stumbled, falling into and against them. I tried to steady us with a foot on one of the lower limbs—maybe even the one that had caught me in the face. Rifka clutched at me with both arms, and I felt my weight shifting. Even as I heard a branch cracking, I felt the boat slip out from under me.

PART FIVE

CHAPTER EIGHTEEN

The boat was gone. Swallowed up in the white infinity. Gone. I pulled us in, toward the tree itself. Another branch cracked—fortunately just a small one, one that had been in the way.

It was like working through a thicket. Then my foot touched solid ground. It was slippery, but I ducked down and worked over thick exposed roots until I could pull Rifka after me.

It was still snowing too heavily to see. We were ashore, and she needed help *now*. She'd lost the bearskin, and her clothes were caked against her body, already iced up and cracking when I moved her. I put my face close to hers and breathed against her mouth, her nose, her eyes. Once her eyes flickered open to stare at me and closed again.

I pulled off my cloth coat, and put it around her. I eased her down into a hunched-over sitting position. When I stood again, the wind drove the snow clear through to my skin.

But that wasn't important.

I could take it; I *had* to take it. I was more than human; I couldn't be hurt. Right? Maybe.

I couldn't close my fingers over the haft of my knife. So I broke handfuls of twigs off the nearby tree barehanded. I threw them down next to Rifka, and when I had more, the first were half-covered with snow. But I gathered still more. Then I knelt over them, my body to the windward side, shielding them, wondering where I'd find a stone to strike against my piece of steel.

I cried, then. My tears froze on my cheeks, but they were real; they were tears of rage, of frustration, of helplessness and fear. The fear was for Rifka, the human whom I loved. I had to have a fire, and I couldn't make one!

I sobbed, and then I coughed, and then I gagged, and as

132

I did a strange warmth began stealing over me, isolating me from wind and cold, and my skin felt tingling and vibrating.

My jaw dropped open and my tongue folded against the bottom of my mouth, *and a stream of fire shot out*.

It carved harmlessly into the air, a thin ruby beam that cut through the white vortex of the snow and vanished beyond sight. I jerked back my head, reflexively, and it dropped, pointing down into the snow, melting the snow wherever it touched it, sizzling the snow into instant steam.

And finally I had the wit to point my head at the pile of twigs.

The ruby ray flickered over the twigs for a single moment, and then they were popping into hungry flames.

And the beam of heat was gone.

Well, I knew how I'd killed that bear, now.

I built up a roaring fire, and then, while Rifka sat in a stupor before it, I began whittling at the tough thicker branches of the tree until I had a sort of hollow carved among them. Then I began taking off my clothes. Fortunately, I'd been wearing a goodly number of layers of clothing. By the time I was finished fastening them to the branches and spreading them out, I had a shelter built, and one which cut off the brunt of the wind.

Now I moved the fire. I simply worked a couple of burning faggots closer to my improvised shelter, and then pushed the others over. Then I picked up Rifka in my naked arms and brought her inside.

The fire was burning well, and the shelter caught and cupped the heat. I took my coat off the girl, and began stripping her. Each piece of her clothing I hung inside the shelter. They would provide more protection from the wind while steaming dry, I hoped. My coat I spread on the slushy ground.

Finally I had Rifka naked. Her skin was bluish, and her breathing very slow and irregular. I was careful not to put her too close to the fire, while I kneaded and worked her skin, rubbing her and massaging her all over. Her skin was very cold.

After a time, she began moving a little, jerking her head about, and mumbling. I put my ear close to her mouth.

"I'm tired . . . why're waking m' up? Le' m' be . . ."

"It's better if you wake up, Rifka," I said gently. But she said nothing more.

Her breathing had improved, though, and when her clothing had begun to dry out, I started redressing her. I kept only her thin coat to wrap around myself.

Night fell. The snow that showed itself beyond the fire was still as heavy as ever. I could see it had become much deeper; its weight bowed down the limbs of our shelter. Sweat rolled off Rifka's brow, and her teeth began chattering again. She had the fever. I could only hope she would get no worse. I wondered what I could do about food. All our provisions had gone with the boat. We were back where we'd started, if not a little worse off.

I stayed awake all that night, staring out at the snow, feeding the fire, and watching over Rifka.

I wished I understood human physiology better. Had she been exposed to the cold too long? What did the fever mean? She writhed and moaned, twisting and turning. Once she tried to tear her clothes off. It jerked at my heart—she was too weak to even pull loose a button. But I was afraid to let her cool again, afraid that if I gave her the relief she wanted, it would only compound her danger.

Instead, I scooped up handfuls of snow and held them to her mouth so that she could lick at the snow and taste driblets of cool water. It seemed to calm her for a time.

Morning was a gradual greying of the darkness beyond the fire. But slowly, as the hours passed, the winds died, and the snow fell more gently. At last, only hours—if my mental clock was not entirely off—from dusk, the snow stopped.

The skies were still leaden and low-hanging. But the air was clear. I could see rolling hills and soft billows, the snow covering everything with thick and gentle curves.

When I stepped out into the snow, I found it was midway to my knee, even in the wind-shadow before the shelter. Beyond, it was over my knees in places.

It was good to stand and stretch again. Before me were hills without distinguishing features, marked only by occasional stands of trees. Behind me . . .

The tree under which we'd taken shelter grew on the very bank of the river. Its roots were writhing fingers where the bank had eroded away from them. Only a little way upstream, the land climbed abruptly into a cliff-like bank that threatened to topple over into the water. The river itself was dark. Fallen branches and debris, washed into projections of the banks, were glistening white arms outthrust into the current. Downstream were more trees, and what looked like a swampy dip in the land, the whiteness of the ground broken in places by black pools.

But no sign of house or habitation.

I selected the tree closest to our sheltering tree, pushed myself through the tangle of its dead lower limbs, and began climbing it.

The view from as high as I dared go was not, at first, any more encouraging. But then my eye lit on a distant hill.

It looked . . . wrong.

It was too round, too regular. I tried to screw up my eyes for a better look. Yes, this was no natural formation. It looked like the upper third of a giant ball. It was snow-covered, and yet . . . and yet . . . I seemed to make out fine networks of criss-crossing straight lines running over its surface.

I had no idea what it could be, but it looked like the only artifact in the entire area. If it would offer shelter, fine. If people lived there, better yet. It made no sense to worry about what *kind* of people might live there. That there might *be* people would be enough.

I climbed down the tree and began scouting for two slender, relatively straight saplings.

I had to descend into the swamp for them. My feet broke through thin crusts of ice and sank into an ooze of mud compounded with many seasons' dead leaves. The saplings grew in a cluster from common roots. I whittled on two until I could hardly see them in the dim light. But finally I felled them. They were of tough, hard wood.

I was frozen through by then, and I dragged the two saplings back to the fire with numb and bleeding fingers.

That night I stayed awake again, keeping the fire burning and working on my two saplings, cutting away all branches and trimming them to a common length. The cuttings went into the fire. They sizzled a bit, but they burned.

The next morning I rigged the travois.

Basically a drag-litter, it consisted of the two poles I'd

135

cut, lashed together at one end and spread in an open V at the other. I ran the poles through Rifka's coat, then bundled her into it, thrusting her arms through the sleeves to keep her from falling out of it. The coat buttons I supplemented by running loose thongs around her body to the poles. Then I took down the shelter, dressing again and drying out my own coat before the fire. My feet were still damp, but warm enough for the moment. When at last I could put it off no longer, I lifted up the joined end of the travois and set out on foot, dragging it behind me. I was headed for the strange dome I'd sighted to the south.

It was slow going. My hands and arms were first to protest. Then I stopped to make a harness arrangement that went over my shoulders and across my chest. That made easier work of pulling the travois, but it was still grueling. I had to lean into my load, often staggering through midthigh drifts, my feet churning without purchase, the load on my back an anchor that sometimes seemed rooted to the spot.

Rifka made no complaint. Most of the time she was in a feverish sleep, her dreams too deep for me to rouse her. From time to time I would stop to hold some snow to her lips, and she would lick at it voraciously, all the while never opening her eyes, never giving any sign that she could hear me or speak to me.

I toiled with a feverishness of my own. I sensed I was running a losing race with death, and it frightened me, made sweat run down inside my clothes, and gnawed at my gut.

How far away could that place be? I'd come only a few miles, but it had consumed most of the day. My legs were lead weights, and as dusk approached once more, I seemed to drift into a dozing sleep, jerking suddenly awake to find myself standing upright, leaning into my harness, and unmoving.

It made no sense to stop for the night. The land was too open to provide shelter, and I mistrusted my ability to start another fire with that strange beam from my mouth. It was better to keep moving, keep shortening the distance between us and——*it*.

The clouds overhead grew feathery, and the night air

136

colder. The moon broke through and the snow became almost as bright as day. I struggled, I slogged, up hill and down, through drifts and across patches scrubbed bare by the wind, mindlessly onward.

The moon was sliding below a western cloudbank when I topped a hill and saw my destination again.

It was still distant, but I could see it more fully now.

It was huge—as big, as broad at the base, as the hill on which I stood.

It was a perfect hemisphere, rising like a half-burned moon out of the very ground itself. Sometimes I thought I saw lights flickering over its surface, but at other times I was convinced they were only the moon's chance beams on the snow.

I lost sight of it again as I descended the hill, but it was still there when I topped the next. It became a game of idiot's hide-and-seek, here now, gone then, back again. I was beyond thinking. I only knew I had a goal, and that I must remain fixed upon it. I forgot the living person riding the travois on my back, I forgot the weight of her. I forgot where I'd come from or where it was I wanted, eventually, to go. I became a machine, geared to a single simple task. *Get to the dome.*

With a jar I realized that the dome stood directly before me. I blinked my eyes. It was vast. It made a wall that climbed high above, and spread to each side as far as I could see. But in the greying pre-dawn light, I could not see far.

I was here!

I staggered a little, aware for the first time in hours of my cold, my fatigue. A door: where was a door?

Still pulling the dead weight of the travois and its burden, I stumbled around to my right and began following the side of the dome. Up close like this, I could see that the side was made up of triangular pieces, their sides joined with long straight struts.

MMMMMMMmmmmmmmmmMMMMMMMMMmmmmmm
mmmMMMMMmmmmMMMMMmmmmm MMmmMMmmMM
MMMmmmmMMMMMmmmmMMMMMMMMMmmmmmmmmm
mMMMMMMMM. . .

Fear washed over me in great throbbing waves.

. . .mmmmmmmmMMMMMMMMmmmmmmmmMM
MMMMMMmmmmMMMM. . .

I stopped, stock still, my muscles frozen, locked in agony.

. . .mmmmMMMmmMMmmMMMMmmmmMMMMMM
MMMmmmmmmmmmMMMMMMMMMmmmmmmmmm. . .

Sóund. It was pure sound. I pushed the thought from the rational part of my mind into the irrational part that was *me.*

. . .MMMMMMMMMmmmmmmmmmMMMMMMMMMMm
mmmmmmmmMMMMMMMMMMmmmmMMMMMmmmmMM
MM. . .

Sound too deep to be heard with my ears. Sound that could only be felt, felt as a basic body throb that created fear.

. . .MMMMMMMMMmmmmmmmmmMMMMMMMMMMm
mmmmmmmmMMMMMMMMMMmmmmMMMMMmmmmMM
MM. . .

Rifka screamed——

. . . mmmmmmmmMMMMMMMMM. . .

——And I broke out of my trance, and threw myself forward, driving my legs like pistons against the snow, pulling and charging like a wild ox.

. . . mmmmmm. . .

The sounds couldn't touch me now. Adrenalin flooded my system. I was plowing through the snow, moving faster than I had managed before.

. . . mmmm.

The pressure faded away, but still I drove on. Then, suddenly, a crisp, clean white blade of light cut across the snow in my path, and I stopped.

A door had opened in the side of the dome. Two men stood there.

Warmth rushed at me through the open doorway, and I swung myself around to enter it.

One of the men held his hand up. "Halt!"

He was wearing a skintight blue suit of fabric that covered him from neck to toe. He wore no weapon, held no weapon. His skin was a burnished brown.

"In," I said. "In."

"You can't come in here, savage. Didn't you feel the warning?"

I nodded. "Yeah. Heard it. Coming in. *Now.*"

"Hardy type," the second remarked. He was dressed identically, only his skin was a little lighter.

"Unusual," the first agreed. "On your way," he said to me. He started to swing the door shut.

I charged. The travois was still on my back, but my knife was in my hand. I lunged, throwing my body hard against the door, battering it open with my combined weight, and falling through.

"*In,* Goddammit!" I shouted. "I'll kill you!"

A red haze had fallen over my eyes and I hardly felt the skin-prickle of the heat around me. I shrugged and shucked my harness loose, the travois falling heavily to the floor. I staggered from the release. We were in some kind of silver-sided room. I didn't notice details. I crouched, my knife held before me. "You die if she dies," I said, jerking my thumb back at the travois. "You put us out, you kill her. But first, I get you." The words came out of my throat in a thick guttural sound.

"Hey, wait now!" the first man said, warily circling away from his companion. "What's this you've got here?"

"Rifka," I said.

In answer, she moaned.

The man's eyes were direct. "What happened to her?"

"She fell in the river," I said, blinking away the fog that was filling my eyes. "In the blizzard. Gotta fever. Bad."

"In the blizzard?" asked the other. "But that was two, three days ago!"

"Waited till snow stopped. Climbed a tree. Saw this thing. Cut poles, made travois. Came here," I said. My legs were weaving under me. I couldn't see the first man at all. His voice came from behind him, and I tried to turn, a growl working in my throat.

"She does look bad," he was saying. He was bending over Rifka. "Exposure, shock, pneumonia . . . ?"

"You gotta help her," I said, and then I passed out.

139

I've often wished there could be a way to forget the winter we spent in New City. But it's impossible. There's too much that I achieved too painfully. Those memories will never leave me again, until I die. And yet, I relive those months as seldom as I can.

Highlights, then——

New City was built in a geodesic dome shortly after Chaos. It was built by a group of Black Separationists, headed by a man remembered only as Elijah. It was designed for two purposes. First, it was to be an enclave for Negroes. And second, it was to be an enclave for scientists, engineers, and technicians.

The personnel was small at the beginning, and the men outnumbered the women five-to-one. The equipment was smuggled and stolen so as to evade the Proctors and sanity enforcements. (The desire to seclude oneself in a private enclave would have been considered un-sane.) When Chaos came, efforts were increased. The dome-city was made self-sufficient by the use of a nuclear-fusion power plant. Hydroponic gardens were built in the upper levels, where transparent plastic plates were used in the dome instead of aluminum.

Breeding was scientifically controlled. The population was stabilized within two hundred years at five hundred men and five hundred women. Intelligence was bred for, and each child was rigorously tested and trained. But, as I soon discovered, a subtle class structure had grown up nonetheless. Those with the darkest skins ranked highest. And a person such as Rifka or myself was regarded as bottom-rung.

Since the Chaos, the inhabitants of New City had discouraged all intercourse with those who lived beyond the limits of their dome. If there had ever been a good reason for it (and there probably was, in the mobs of looters who poured out of the cities after Chaos began), it was long forgotten. It was only the humanitarian instincts of the two who had guarded the door that had allowed us entrance.

That was impressed upon me at the beginning.

The man peering down at me was seven feet tall and his skin was blue-black. His jumpsuit was coal-black. His white teeth glittered at me as he spoke, and his speech was as precise as that of the Com-Comp.

"You represent an unusual case, Mr. Tanner," he said. His voice was very deep, perfectly modulated, and rolled over me with an inexorable finality. "You are the first white man—the first stranger of any kind, in fact—whom we have allowed in our city for well over seventy-five years."

I gave him a weak smile. I was lying in a bed in a sterile-looking room, and I had no doubt of my status. I'd tested my sheets. They were fastened to hold me pinned down as surely as if I was bound with ropes. "Once every seventy-five years, you let in starving blizzard victims, huh?"

"I'm not here to make jokes with you, Mr. Tanner. That is not my province. My interest in you was initially aroused by your primitive ferocity in defending your mate. It isn't every day we have the chance to study one of your kind, you know. In fact, it's been years since we've been approached by anything but a stray cow or two . . ."

"What's happened to Rifka?" I asked. "How is she?"

"Touching," he murmured. "Quite touching. All those primitive emotions, excitements. You seem quite attached to the girl. Well, you may rest more easily. She seems to be recuperating quite well."

"What did you do to her——and to me?" I asked.

"Only simple germicidal sterilizing techniques. We removed all your hair—an excellent transporter of disease—and irradiated your skin surfaces. We can't have you bringing all sorts of viruses and bacteria in here, can we? Blood tests; toxication. Very simple, very ordinary. We took a few radiographs, too." His voice took on a hard edge and I wondered what was coming. It was an obvious buildup.

"Mr. Tanner, *why do you have steel bones?*"

"The blood test was what alerted us," Dr. Meskin explained to me, later. He was short, balding, deep brown. He smiled often, and it was easy to like his bedside manner. "Even we, although we control our environment almost one hundred per cent, even we have bacteria in our bodies. We've never entirely licked viral diseases either. But your blood sample, well! To begin with, it began clotting almost immediately, and we had to introduce an agent to reduce the clotting factor. Then we found that while your blood was completely free of trace infection, it was amazingly alive. It teemed with antibodies, it thrived, it refused to lie down and die! Why, I almost thought it would grow into another one of you and rise right up off my microscopic viewing station. Just amazing! Healthiest blood I've *ever* seen. So we thought we ought to make a few more tests, just for curiosity's sake. We were sure we had a mutant of some sort on hand, some sort of sport, or a new breed, we weren't sure, but it seemed like an exciting new discovery. That's when we sent word on up to His Honor, Mr. Black. And then we set up X-ray equipment, and, well. . . . You certainly handed us a surprise on *that* one, I will say! Your bones were *shaped* like human bones, but the radiograph plate showed an absolutely solid shadow on each and every one. We did a minor bit of explorative surgery, and verified the point. Stainless steel! In fact, a very fine vanadium alloy. I don't expect anyone was too surprised at the speed with which you healed again after we closed you up." His smile was warm. "Frankly, I just don't know what to make of you, Mr. Tanner. Nobody ever grew up with steel bones——not unless they've invented organic-alloy steel. You're nobody's mutant. What you look like to me is, somebody has been messing around trying to invent the Better Human Being. And you're *it*.

"Now who in hell has that kind of technology in a world like this one? Hmmm?"

"Back to the same question, huh?"

"I'm afraid so."

"What if I told you I don't know——that I have no memories more than a couple months old?"

"Well, I'm not sure I'd believe you."

"You'll have to live with it. I do."

Meskin stood up. On him even the standard one-piece orange jumpsuit managed to look rumpled. "I just don't know," he said, shaking his head. "I just can't figure what to do with you."

"While you're thinking about it, could I see Rifka—the girl I brought in with me?"

He frowned. "Don't see why not. She's pretty healthy now. Just a normal human being, you know . . . none of your fancy stuff in her. Pregnant, nothing else."

"Pregnant? You mean, carrying a baby?"

"Umm-hm," he nodded, absently.

"For how long? I mean, how old is it?"

"Oh . . . a month, less than a month, I guess. She probably didn't even know herself."

"It's—all right?"

"She's basically healthy."

"But the cold, the shock——?"

"No harm that I could see."

I thought back: we'd made love for the first time only a little over a month ago.

I sat across a plastic desk from His Honor, Mr. Black, again. I wore a white jumpsuit. It fit me embarrassingly like a second skin.

"Mr. Tanner," he said, his deep voice shaping each syllable mellifluously. "We've had you under observation now for two months."

"You've had me caged up here for two months, you mean," I said. "And so far I've played along with you. But there are limits."

"You've gone along with our physical testing program, you mean, but you balk at our new mental program."

"The tests were fun, in a roundabout sort of way. It was nice to establish my, ah, competency at so many things." They'd defined my limits for me, and at every turn I could tell I had them running scared, although they would not admit it. I was just a little bit too much better than they—with their centuries of scientific breeding and training—could be. And none of their tests had released my trigger and thrown me into overdrive——yet. That was one trick I wanted to remain my private secret.

"But you are unwilling to let us tap your memories."

"How do I know what you'd do to my brains once you had me wired up?"

"Mr. Tanner." He let his voice get a little impatient. "You've protested to us all along that you have no memory of how you came to be, no memory that extends back more than a few months, even. Aren't *you* even curious? Or"——his voice got hard——"are you lying to us?"

I sighed. "I've told you no lies." Just not all I guessed to be the truth . . .

"Tomorrow morning, Mr. Tanner. Tomorrow morning, you understand? We've played games with you quite enough."

That night I talked with Rifka. We lay together, our heads close, whispering. It seemed possible that listening devices had been planted to eavesdrop on us, but I doubted they'd try to overhear us now.

"How do you feel?" I asked.

"Very nice," she said, her smile warm and smug. She patted her belly. There was the barest bulge. Considering her diet in this place, I wasn't sure it couldn't be explained as a few more pounds gained. "Both of us." Her eyes twinkled with delight. "You see," she added, "you truly are a man."

If it's mine, I almost said. But I didn't see how it could be anyone else's. Sometimes it bothered me. On other occasions I would recall the hollow, echoing voice of the Com-Comp: *"You have been cloaked with completely human flesh and organs."* Had that been only a dream . . . or something more?

"I'm afraid——of tomorrow," I said.

"The tests?"

"Yes."

"But maybe it would help. Maybe it would tell you what you want to know."

"Maybe." I shivered. "But maybe I'd be better off *not* knowing."

"Why?"

"I'm not sure . . . some dreams I've had. Maybe real memories, maybe just dreams. If they're real . . . well, I don't think I *should* know."

"Dreams? Which dreams?"

"I don't really want to talk about them."

144

"Oh. I'm sorry."

"Oh, hey," I said, mussing with her short frizzy hair. It was still a shock to look at her each time; such short reddish hair, like a boy. I'd gotten pretty mad the first time I'd set eyes on her. We'd both been shaved bald. Now we could laugh about it. "I'm sorry. Don't get hurt. Come on, now." I stroked her a little, and she snuggled closer in my arm, and we caressed each other gently.

But all the while, a tight knot gathered in my gut, as I wondered what they'd find——and hoped they'd fail.

I was stripped, and then fitted into a device that held me in a reclining position. Straps and wires were fixed to different parts of my body, and a cap went over my head. *It was all very pleasantly reminiscent of something else . . .*

I felt pinpricks in my scalp. "We've had to make a lot of modifications," Meskin's voice said distantly. He was explaining. "X-rays showed that his cranium was steelcapped and enclosed, but part of it, below the frontal lobes, was segregated into a separately enclosed section. The arrangement doesn't appear to exactly coincide with the normal brain schema."

A high thin whine began. I heard it less than I felt it.

"We're boring now, to a distance of thirteen sixty-fourths of an inch. That should bring our probes within about three sixty-fourths of complete penetration."

I felt something clamp, delicately but precisely, into my head . . .

"The probes are in . . ."

. . . And blackness washed up over me.

I was in a grim cell. It was barred, like a cage, and the door clinked shut behind me with metallic finality. I had four cellmates.

The closest was a skinny-looking kid of maybe sixteen. His blond hair was untrimmed, and his eyes stayed on the floor. Next to him, lying on the bench, was a little boy. He was curled into a fetal ball, sucking his thumb and crying.

On the opposite bench, a dark young man, staring evenly at me with hostile eyes. He sized me up, decided I was no help to him in my wounded condition, and looked away.

The fourth was huddled in the corner and at first I

*overlooked him. Then he began moaning, his voice build-
ing into a scream that built in pitch until it hurt my ears,
and then fell once more to silence.*

*The fear in this cell was thick in the air. I could smell it
amid the other smells. The little boy had wet himself. He
might not be alone.*

*This was a cell for the condemned. We were all enemies
of the state, deviants, the Unsane. There was no room for
us in a sane society. Soon we would be executed. Soon we
would be dead.*

*How did it feel to be a little boy and know you were
going to die? How could he know life? But that was the age
they got most deviants. That was when most of them
showed up on the brain scanners——age six to sixteen
That's when the neuroses, the psychoses, the rebellion, the
deviation came out.*

*Deviation was not to be tolerated. A sane society had
been set up, and a mechanism to keep it pure. I alone had
not fallen victim to the ubiquitous encephalogrammatic
scanners.*

I had steel limbs. I was physically deviant.

*A shotgun blast had torn open my side, exposing my
steel rib cage, and yet I lived. But no one was curious. No
one cared. It wasn't sane to be curious. It wasn't healthy.*

*They came for us. Two Proctors for each of us. We were
each asked if we wished to be blindfolded for the final walk.
We all refused. I don't think the one in the corner had even
heard. The small boy came sniffling to his feet, and gave his
hand to an elderly Proctor. I wondered what thoughts
passed through the man's mind as he led a trusting little boy
to his death. A Proctor grabbed each shoulder, and they
hauled the moaning one from the corner. He let out fresh
wails.*

*It was an afternoon execution. They took us through so
many corridors it was a sick joke. Finally we were at a pair
of black doors.*

*Beyond those doors, the Arena. Once a theatre, where
the Unregulated watched moving pictures of vicarious
violence, satisfying their sickness. Now an Arena, where the
Regulated did their duty as citizens. One thousand seats,
one thousand pushbuttons. Who knew how many were
wired into the circuit? One, some, many, all? Responsibility*

became anonymous. No one was guilty; all were guilty.

There was no ceremony to it, just business as usual. We were marched through the doors and out onto the floor, once a stage. The moaning one was shrieking himself hoarse. The little boy was crying again.

A full house. It always was.

They strapped us into chairs, and fastened electrodes to our bodies. Caps went over our heads. A special seat went inside the bigger seat for the little boy.

"May all your children enjoy the same," I said bitterly to the Proctor holding the boy down. "Too bad it didn't happen to your mother." But he ignored me. He'd heard them all before. It was just his job. After all he didn't push the button. Proctors never pushed the buttons. They alone were guiltless.

The lights dimmed once in warning. In the front row I saw a fat man. I knew he was familiar, but I couldn't place him. He was staring at me. Many took their own pleasure in peering at us, trying to fathom our unsanity, trying to understand the gap that placed us down on the floor, and they up in the seats. There was a subtle irony here . . . I'd been in those seats myself, only three days earlier.

And now the little blue lights were about to snap on. I could feel the fingers poised over their buttons, like a thousand swords over my head.

Someone made contact. I felt my muscles contract in a spasm of rigidity. My nostrils were full of the smell of searing flesh: mine. Everything before my eyes flashed white——then——black——then white in increasingly rapid alternation. Then the red knife of pain cut through all the rest.

CHAPTER TWENTY

"We had to stop," Meskin told me. "You were about to destroy the fittings."

"What was I doing?" I asked. I was flat on my back in a hospital bed again. It felt like the one I'd had before.

"Ah, well, I don't think we'd best speak of it just now," Dr. Meskin said soothingly.

"Look, Meskin, I remember it as well as you do——the part your machine dredged up, I mean. Very efficient, that machine." I couldn't keep the edge of bitterness from my voice.

"Ahh, yes," Meskin sighed. "I suppose you must. The memories of death . . . very traumatic, I should think. Unpleasant; not to be remembered under ordinary circumstances. I can see why you repressed them."

"What did I do?" I repeated.

"Well, at the, ah, um, precise moment, your memories stimulated a . . . reenactment, I guess we might call it."

"In simple words, Doctor?"

"You went through the same, uh, death spasms again."

I closed my eyes and tried to keep it from overwhelming me again while I thought. An execution: it tied in. In my dream, the one in the castle that had been so real, the Com-Comp had mentioned an execution. How did it go again? *"The last real action you undertook was . . . your execution."* What had followed? Why wasn't I dead? *"Your body has been repaired, and is now functional."*

And, *"You were constructed as a data-gathering device."* How had the Com-Comp put it when I'd been awakened in that little metal cell? *"You are an artificially constructed human being, a mobile data-gathering device."*

Steel bones. Human flesh and organs. It checked. I was a construct. I'd known that all along, although not the details. But for what purpose? *What had been my original purpose?*

"Those were obviously pre-Chaos memories, Mr. Tan-
148

ner. Very vivid. Better than any record we have, as an indication of the inhuman savagery of white society in that period." Black stood over me as they strapped me in for another run. "Now, *what are you doing with pre-Chaos memories?*"

"Perhaps his brain was preserved, for implantation in this body. Suspended animation, perhaps? Cryogenics?" suggested Meskin. They carefully fitted my head in the preselected position and lowered the cap again. *I knew now what this reminded me of.*

"No," said Black. "He was steel-boned then, just as he is now. His own body impressions are subjective, of course, but I doubt he was occupying a different body, or, if he was, if that one was much different from this. It was wounded, remember? But he was still strong, still surprisingly healthy."

"Like an ox," Meskin chuckled. "Still, I wouldn't be surprised if this whole routine isn't unpleasantly suggestive . . . a cap, wires . . ."

Black snorted. "Let's get on with it. This man is an enigma, a scientific riddle. I want him solved."

So do I, you bastard, I thought. *So do I.*

I was sitting in a lush apartment. Facing me was a girl with red hair. I recognized her instantly. She was the girl I'd known in my dreams.

"*But, what does the complex want?*" she was saying. "*All those hallucinations you had . . . ?*"

"*I'm supposed to do something,*" I told her. "*The complex can't give me directions. That would be seizing the initiative, meddling in human affairs. It can't do that. It's not programmed to.*"

"*But what, then?*"

"*Those hallucinations were meant to show me things. The first gave me an inside-out picture of the world this would be without the complex, without the scanners and enforced sanity. It was a mad world, falling apart at the seams, and yet, the people were* alive. *Very few people in this world strike me as alive in that sense, Hoyden. Very few.*"

She slumped. "*I know what you're going to say. Why haven't I been picked up? This luxurious apartment, hidden away in a warehouse, the paintings, the liquor, all that sort of thing——how do I rate?"*

"A good question: How have you escaped the brain scanners?"

"I think you know."

"Your father."

She nodded. *"It happened back when they set the whole complex up. It was originally just a computerized information center, you know. It was designed to monitor the scanners. Later on, they added all the other services. It runs the whole country now——subways, planes, everything.*

"Daddy—he was the head of the project. He called together the top administrators, there were four of them. And he asked them what they thought their chances were of surviving; theirs and their families'."

"So they programmed the complex so that specific brain patterns, their encephalic waves and those of their families, would be automatically skipped over by the scanners," I said.

She agreed. *"I've never had to be afraid of the scanners. I was born after they were functioning; I was a change-of-life baby. But Daddy programmed me in. I've felt so . . . so guilty about it, knowing that I was living a life no one around me could live. It's done things to us, to all of us. I've known for years we'd all be picked up tomorrow if we weren't immune. Do you know what it's like, staring at other people and knowing, 'He could get picked up for thinking the thoughts I'm thinking'?"*

I nodded. *"I'm immune too."*

"You are?"

"The complex reprogrammed my I.D. No one will ever know I was executed. No one will even care. I'm back where I started, before I knew any of this: a data-gathering arm of the complex."

"More than that," she said.

"Yes."

"But what?"

I was talking about the hallucinations I had, while the complex was putting me back in shape again. I told you, they were very real, even the last sequence."

"The one in Eden?"

150

"For what it was, yes. It too was supposed to tell me something."

"Tell me."

"We've made a farce of 'sanity.' Sure, we've built a nicely ordered little world. No slums, no poverty, no neglect. No overpopulation either. Did you know that something like thirty-five per cent of the total population is seized for execution?"

She jammed her fingers in her mouth. *"That's horrible,"* she said softly.

"It can't go on," I said. *"Our race is stagnating and dying. We're breeding out creativity and intelligence and sensitivity. We're breeding a race of automatons. Compulsive sanity of the sort we have now does not lead to real mental health. There's no happiness in being a vegetable."*

"What can you do?"

"Wipe the slate clean," I said. *"This world must go."*

"I'm scared," I said.

Rifka tightened her arms around me. "Why?"

"Because they know enough now, if they only realize it. And because I know too much."

"Too much? *What* do you know?"

"I know who——and what——I am now," I said.

"I don't know if I can take any more of this," I told them.

"Nonsense. You must. We are very close to the core of the problem now."

"Look, Black: for you it's just another scientific undertaking, an intellectual exercise. For me, it's gut-wrenching. You're reaching into me with those probes of yours and you're pulling out bits and pieces of *me—and it hurts.*"

"He's undoubtedly right," Meskin agreed with me. "These are strongly repressed memories—it's not hard to see why—and most naturally those fighting strongest for release. That's the nature of what our machine finds. It breaks down electro-chemical inhibiting neuro-bonds, and whatever has been locked away most firmly—that's what comes out first. These memories represent deep traumas. I

151

strongly doubt that Mr. Tanner is enjoying them."

"We are not here to discuss the ways and means of providing for Mr. Tanner's enjoyment," Black said acidly. "We are here to discover just what it is that Mr. Tanner *is*. And *I* find these memories of his fascinating beyond experience. I've already made a notation to have the tapes permanently preserved in the main library."

"You're a vulture," I said.

"Your vocabulary is broadening a good bit," Black remarked. "You see, even you are profiting by this experiment."

I was running across a broad surface, burnished bright copper in the sunlight.

I was on the roof of the gigantic computer-complex. The shimmering expanse was vast, covering many city blocks. But I was approaching a nearby edge, close to which was parked a hovercraft. Hoyden's father was struggling to pitch his daughter into the cockpit.

The roof was smooth, hard to keep my footing on. I was afraid to run too fast. The two were slipping and grappling far too close to the precipitous edge.

"Hoyden!" I shouted, fear gripping me. "Get back! Stay away from the edge!"

Her father looked up and saw me. He was fat, a gross caricature of a man. He'd been the man at my execution; I knew him now. He snarled at me, lips drawn back away from his teeth like a rat's. Then, without warning, he threw his daughter at me. Her flaming hair whipped across my face, blinding me. I caught her, then pulled free.

The fat man ran straight off the roof's edge.

The sun's rays beat down on us like hammers, and bounced back up at us to dance in our eyes. A chill breeze moved across the rooftop, tugging at Hoyden's skirt. She clutched at my hand. It was a little like being on a mountaintop.

On hands and knees, I peered over the edge.

Far below green treetops rippled gently, like wavelets in a pool. I used my vision to zoom up on the scene directly below.

The concrete walk ran a border around the Complex

152

Building of gleaming white, the trees casting vivid blue shadows across it. On the spot directly below, the white was smeared with red.

I pulled back. "Dead," I said. "It's finished now. Don't look."

She pulled my arm around her and shuddered. "He—just jumped off! Why? Why did he do that?"

I shook my head. "I don't know," I said. "The sun, maybe. It might have gotten in his eyes. It's tricky up here. Or maybe it was the knowledge that he wasn't going to be immune any longer. He's been to enough executions. He probably didn't want to go to another."

I led her across the roof to the stairs that led back down into the central programming room. Our arms were around each other's waists, and she was warm against me.

"It's time for a new beginning," I said. "It's time to reprogram the complex. And this time for Chaos."

"*You* were the one," said Black. His voice was low, controlled, emotionless. It gave no hint to his thoughts.

"Yes," I said. "I was the one."

"But, *why?*" asked Meskin. "Why, man?"

"There's an old saying," I said. " 'You can't make an omelette without breaking eggs.' " I remembered it all, now. I knew it all. The knowledge lay heavy on me, and I did not want to sit here, in Black's office, explaining myself, justifying myself to him.

I was the Death Machine. Or rather, the Com-Comp —the computer-complex, to give it its true name——and I were the Death Machine. *We* built and programmed the robots to go out and scatter the people into the forests and wilderness. *We* cut all services, destroyed opposition, let the sheep die.

Survival of the fittest. That was the process of evolution, wasn't it? And what had man done, with his computer-enforced 'sanity' but bypass that process? It had become *survival of the most sheeplike.* The race was dying.

Which was better? Slow death or quick? Most of the sane citizenry was never alive. How then might they die now? And those who did *not* die——? *They* were the fit. They would survive. Perhaps not many, at first. But some. Always some.

153

The complex had run some figures on it. Of the world's remaining five billion 'sane,' less than one per cent were likely to survive. In highly urbanized areas, the figure was closer to one-tenth of one per cent. By 1950, there were over a billion people in the world. It had taken all mankind's history to build to that number. Less than one hundred years later, the world population doubled, and there were over two billion. In thirty years, there were *three* billion. Before the dawn of 'regulated sanity' there were over seven billion. The population had fallen then, and stabilized.

But after Chaos, few would survive. First would come the breakdown of credit, and anarchy. Then famine, fires, and then plagues. The four horsemen would gallop over the world, and for many it would be the Apocalypse.

I'd watched it happen. From copters flying overhead, I'd monitored it on screens within the complex. I'd watched the maddened mobs rage, destroying themselves. I'd watched the great fires sweep over Chicago, Tokyo, Peking, London. I'd watched the great American Breadbasket swept by the worst prairie fire of all time. Forests fell. Cities toppled. And everywhere the people ran, ducking and darting, like tiny ants, waiting for the boot to smash them.

I wore the boot.

Could any man accept such responsibility? I knew it was the right move, but could I accept its immediate consequences?

It was after Hoyden stole a copter and ran away that I asked the complex to turn me off.

"I've served my purpose," I told it. "Do whatever it is you must do. I don't want to live any more."

"A time may come when you might be needed again."

"I don't want to know about it. You must promise me: I mustn't remember. I must have no memories. Hoyden's——gone. The Earth is in flames. I have nothing to be proud of."

"On the contrary. You have done much to save Man from himself. You have successfully served your purpose."

There are no memories beyond that point.

They let us go in the spring.

I can't say they were bad hosts. There are others I didn't

154

mention: Nichole, of the sad soft eyes; Palmer, slender, curious, amusing, amateur psychiatrist; Williamson, hard-science man with a need to know what made me tick, physically; Ebertson; Bronson; Shorter; Delany; all the others who tried to find ways to understand me, to like me, or to help me. They filled my time with themselves. By the time we left, we were no longer inferior white people, primitives, backsliders. I was a celebrity, Rifka was accepted.

Perhaps she was better liked than I; I can't tell. There was always the thing of Chaos between myself and the others. Chaos did not mean to them quite what it had to the rest of the world. It hastened their withdrawal, but did not cause it. Perhaps it eased the pressure on them. They bore me no malice.

Instead, it seemed, they almost pitied me.

"Goodbye, Mr. Tanner, Rifka," His Honor, Mr. Black, said, taking my hand. Beyond the door was the airlock, and beyond that, springtime. "I wish you well."

We thanked him. It seemed to me I saw a spot of moisture in the corner of his eye. But I didn't look at it. I took Rifka's hand and led her through the door.

We left, as seemed to be our custom, far better equipped than we'd entered. We wore the one-piece jumpsuits as basic garments, and over them, well-laundered and freshly sewn, the clothes we'd worn before. "It may still get cold again, you know. It's only April. It could still snow," Dr. Meskin had said in urging all the clothes on us. "Best you be well-prepared. I've packed rain-slicks, ponchos, they were called, in your bags. Good for rain *or* snow. And good fire-lighters with plenty of fuel . . . I wish we had some kind of transportation for you."

"I think we'll manage. We came most of the way this far on foot," I said. "Maybe we'll even try our luck with the river again, who knows?"

The sun had that newborn, tender warmth you only find in the spring. And fresh green grass was poking shyly up through the winter's dead stalks. Beside me, Rifka was proudly pregnant. She had been assured she was healthy and without complications. "Plenty of walking and fresh air will be good for you," Meskin had assured her. "Don't slouch. Keep good posture. That pack on your back should help. Here are some pills. I've explained them to Tanner. Good luck, and—may you have a boy," he'd concluded shyly.

The air had a fresh smell to it. Somewhere hidden in the grass a bird was warbling. Rifka smiled at me, then laughed. "It's so good to be *out* again! You know?"

I nodded and tried to smile. "Yes," I said. "It's nice."

PART SIX

CHAPTER TWENTY-ONE

It was a tough grade. Archer and I stood face to face, pitching cordwood into the firebox. The muscles stood out in bold relief on his arms, across his chest and shoulders. His skin was covered by a sheen of sweat. His hair was on his shoulders and across his face. He was grinning.

"You still like railroading, Tanner?" he shouted. "Hah?"

The little locomotive chugged furiously with its load of five boxcars and three—almost four—people. We were in the Rockies, and the grades were steep. Twice a day we had to stop the train and get out our axes for fresh wood. At certain rivers, marked on Archer's map, we stopped to take on water. ("It's a closed system, regenerative, and theoretically fully retrievable, but, hell! You ever see a truly closed system, Tanner? We lose water. Sure, not like they did on the Old steam roads, but we lose it.")

We'd met Archer and his railroad train a hundred miles west of the Mississippi River. We'd been following his rail-line for most of that way when one morning we saw smoke on the distant horizon, and late that afternoon the rails began to sing, and in the evening we flagged him down.

Archer was a big man: the biggest I'd met. He stood six-eight and weighted 350, by his own account—"It runs in the family, my man!"—and it looked like it was all muscle. His long hair was straw-colored, sun-bleached, and his skin was deeply tanned. He laughed a lot. He was afraid of no man, and for all I could see, he would never need be.

His fantastic railroad was the quixotic concept of his grandfather, he told me. "Ol' Grand Dad decided the people needed civilizing. 'A man ain't civilized,' he told me once, 'unless he got contact with other men.' Those were pretty savage days east of the Rockies, you know. Well, Granpa, he spent most of his life, resetting this road. He

157

was a wandering man, started out a peddler and medicine man. Got so's people looked forward to his coming, for the news and what-not. He found this railroad yard in Wyoming, and that gave him his idea. Most of the railroad tracks were pretty far gone, but he fitted himself out with a little switcher, converted it to burn wood, did himself a lot of fancy brass plumbing work to hold the steam, and then set out to work himself up a gang to rebuild a road.

"Grades were still there, you know. Some washed out, but all surveyed, all laid in an' everything. Rail was his tough problem, but there was a lot of usable steel and iron lying around the country, and it was just a matter of setting up some sorta foundry to work it. Well, my Ol' Grand Dad, he did it all. Didn't get much fun outta the road before he died, but Pop took it over and did all right. And now she's mine."

The train stopped at scattered communities across the great open grasslands. And here we watched a master at work.

He'd blow the big steam whistle ("One time I don't mind wastin' a little!"), and when he pulled to a stop at the edge of each little town, it seemed as though the entire population was there to greet him. People clapped their hands over their heads and cheered and beat on old tubs and pails to set up a clangor, and little boys jumped up on the wooden cars, climbing onto their roofs while mothers wailed in anguish for them. Dogs—tamer ones, these, although the sight of them still scared Rifka—barked and leapt into the air, full of the excitement.

Then Archer would step up on the little car that held the stacked cordwood, and he'd make his spiel:

"Well, all *right,* now! All *right!* Yes indeed! I surely am glad to see all your happy smiling faces again this trip, and I betcha yore not that sad to see mine——" Laughter.

"What I got fer ya! I got that special chinaware you lady folks prize so much, come straight from where they make it best——Jefferson City! Yeah?"

It was like a call-and-response. He was a preacher, a spellbinder, leading his happy congregation. "Yeah?" he'd ask, and the answer was overwhelming: the men would roar lustily, the women clap and laugh delightedly.

158

"And I got some of that fine suthurn can molasses for you!

"And I got some fine carbon steel knives, what they make in Pine Bluffs!

"And I got——"

He would stand there chanting, reeling off lists of goods and items, everything from hardware ("And I got good straight *nails*, the kind you really pound! They don't bend, they drive true all the way! An' they come from Scott City, now! Yeah?") to staple food items to cosmetics for the ladies. He brought color, life, and excitement into the dull lives of these hard-toiling people, and they loved him for it.

Once he was finished with the chanting, he'd leap down to the ground, and he'd call out, "Now all who's interested, jest form the line!" And over half the menfolk would make a long line, each explaining his needs, offering his trade goods, and striking his bargain with the blond giant.

"Don't you keep a record?" I asked him after the first time. "Written down, I mean?"

"Well, now, I *could*—I kin read an' write, you know. But I got a good head and it ain't failed me yet. I reckon when it does, I'll think on that."

Then he'd slide open the boxcar doors and begin parceling out the goods. Sometimes this took time. Some men traded heavily, and would bring wagonloads with them, taking new wagonloads away again. But Archer was patient, smiling, sweat beading on his bare back as he did the greatest share of loading and unloading.

I helped too: it was our fare across the country. I did what he told me, and tried to help whenever I could, but I got the impression he was letting me pitch in more to make me feel useful than because he really needed me.

Then, after the trading was done, there would be a big community cookout and dinner, dancing, and another kind of line would form before the big man.

"My Johnny, he's been puny lately, and I wonder if you could——?"

"Say no more, ma'am; I surely will take a look at him in the morning."

"I wonder, now, how are they doin' down south? I heard they got a lotta rain at plantin' time."

" 'S a fact, they did, and I'll tell you here and now, it would delight me to be able to take some wheat, some corn down to them come harvest time. I know they'll be a-needing it."

"I am glad to hear you say that; it looks like a bumper year here for us."

"Mister Archer, I'd like you to meet my daughter, Grace; she's just sixteen this week."

"Well, now, she is a right purty thing; takes after her mother, don't she? I wonder if I might have the pleasure of a dance with you, Grace?"

Later, I asked him, "Why haven't you married yet, Archer? It seems as though every mother in every town has hopes you'll marry her daughter."

"They fancy I'm a rich man," Archer said, laughing. "But I'll let you in on a secret—two secrets. For one, I ain't rich. Oh, I make a little something on my trading, sure. But it just pays to keep the railroad going. You don't see 'em, but I got a man, mebbe two, in every town who takes care of my rails in his area. And I gotta give each man something for his time, right? As for the other, don't you go telling none of these people, but I *got* me a wife. Got two, back in Sequoia. And I'll be damned happy to see this trip end, just so's I can spend a little time with 'em." He chuckled broadly.

"*Two* wives?" Rifka had asked, sceptically.

"I'm a big man; there's enough for two, at *least*," Archer laughed. "Besides, lotsa men got a couple wives in Sequoia. That's the way they are. More women than men anyway."

We were heading for Sequoia. "Most beautiful place in all the world," Archer assured us. "Nicest people, too." But it was going slowly. We were following old railroad routes through the mountains, but the grades were steep, and it took both of us working hard to keep the steam up. "Got a heavier load this time, too," Archer grunted.

"*Log!*" Rifka shouted from up in the cab.

Archer made it up to the controls in one jump. He threw the steam bypass valve, and set the brakes. The train screeched to a shuddering halt.

Only a few hundred feet uptrack a log lay across the tracks.

"Don't like the looks of this," Archer muttered. He

reached his hand into a nook in the cab and pulled free a rifle. He checked the action, and remarked, "Semi-auto; real antique. Shoots good." He wasn't smiling. "You, Rifka, stay down, outta sight. Tanner, I dunno. I ain't got another gun up here. How're you with that toad-sticker?"

"You were passed out the night in Platte I won the throwing contest," I said, "but you should've heard about it."

"Yeah, right." He brushed his hair back from his forehead. "Forgot that. Wonder what's holding 'em up?"

"Who?"

"Whoever threw down that log. Don't look like no fallen tree, does it?"

"Why don't I climb down and try moving it off? You cover me with your gun."

"You? That's a big-looking log."

"So maybe I'm little next to you," I said. "I'm not weak."

He nodded. "Try it. But if you see or hear of anything, you drop flat."

I descended to the ground and walked along the embankment. Tough thick grass all but hid the old cinders. The new ties looked like false white teeth among the rotten. Steep slopes rose on my left and fell away to the right. Below was a mountain stream running through the bottom of the chasm. The trees were mostly pines, bright green tufts on the end of their dark green branches. I watched the trees on my left closely. I saw nothing, heard nothing. The woods were silent. Too silent.

The log was rotted. Places on each end showed fresh scars where they'd been gripped. Someone *had* carried this log unto the tracks. As I rolled it, the underside came up, dirt-flecked and still damp. *Recently*.

I was tense. I decided to roll the log off on the uphill side. If men came out of the trees, it might give me a little protection.

The log hung for a moment on the edge of the embankment, and then rolled down into the ditch.

As if that had been a signal, a shot broke the crisp silence, and I felt a heavy hand pick me up under my left shoulder and kick me around. Something wet screamed past my ear in the same second.

I fell into the ditch, rolling over the log. I looked back over the tracks and saw men leaping up from the other side, from the downslope, firing their guns at the train.

There were four of them, and if Archer had been alone, they might have been enough, that is, if it had been he, instead of me, who'd taken that first shot in his shoulder.

From over the boiler of the engine came a sudden fierce staccato, and two of the attackers stumbled and sprawled across the tracks. The third kept running toward the train, firing his rifle and pumping shells into it as he ran. Archer fired again, and spots of blood stitched themselves across the man's back as the bullets tore through him.

The fourth man had dropped and was squirming across the tracks in my direction. I came to my feet and drew my knife.

His head swiveled toward me, and then his mouth dropped open. He made no attempt to raise his rifle or to point it at me. He just stared at me.

My knife in his neck dropped him.

Archer came running up the trackbed, rifle in hand. "God, man—thought he'd got you!" Then he stumbled to a halt and his eyes grew large. "Sheeet!" he said, his breath coming out in a low whistle.

The bullet had gone through muscle and flesh in my shoulder, struck a steel bone, and torn out its exit near my neck in a very messy fashion. I didn't look good.

Archer wanted me to bunk down, in the living car, but I refused. I agreed I wouldn't help feed the firebox for a while, but insisted that once Rifka had washed out the exit wound and bound it up I'd be all right.

"Why did those men attack us, though?" I asked.

"Why does any one think he can get what others worked for without his having to work?" Archer replied. "They was after whatever goods I had, I reckon. It's pretty common knowledge that I do a good bit of trading." He laughed, the first time he had since he'd seen the log. "Guess they got the short end on that trade! Got me some more rifles, ammunition. And they got a quick trip to hell." He sobered. "Good thing, I guess, you were along, Tanner. I sure am sorry about you getting hit."

The mountains, coming as they did after barren desert and endless miles of sandy clay and scrub, were green, cool, and beautiful in their awesomeness. They dwarfed the mountains of the east into hills by comparison. They lost their heads in the clouds, and many were still snow-peaked. But the scenery wasn't enough. I'd used the work, and my fascination for Archer, to keep my mind from brooding, but now that I was inactive again there was no way to avoid it.

Rifka could not understand. She was full with child, and her thoughts too were full of child. She was happy, radiant, and often laughing. She would try to cheer me, to tease me, sometimes tickling me under my ribs or running a wisp of her hair across the soles of my feet, or pull little jokes on me——none of it worked. At night she would crawl close against me, take my hand, and place it against her swollen belly. "Feel him, Tanner? Feel how he kicks! So full of life, he is," she'd say softly but excitedly.

Pregnancy had done something for her. It had changed her looks—her skin glowed, now; and she washed often and with pleasure—until I hardly recognized the ragged creature I'd first known in her. It had changed her thinking too. Gone was the primitive who lived each day without thought for those that had passed or those to come. She was full of plans for the child, full of concern for the past, and full of curiosity for everything around her and everyone we met.

I loved her. Do not forget this. I found her more beautiful every day, and her intellectual growth presented me with pleasant new surprises often. It was like watching a girl-child grow into a woman. I felt an almost paternal pride in her.

But there were those other memories . . .

What had first attracted me to this waif, this Rifka? She had reminded me of another redhead, the girl I'd known once long before, before the Chaos. And now I remembered that girl with the improbable name of Hoyden—her sick father's joke that she had tried, in her own way, to live up to. And I remembered that we too had been in love.

When it had finally come home to her, the immensity of what I had unleashed upon the world——when the meaning of Chaos was clear to her——she told me she could

163

love me no more. I could remember now her parting words:

"You—you're a metal-boned travesty of a human being! And you're more unsane than any of us! You talk about your concern for humanity, but what about *people?* Those little things running around out there, those little tiny dots on your monitor screens, *each one is a real human being.* Each one is a person, caught up in the death of his world. And *you* killed it. You've killed his mother and his father and his sister, and before you're done, he'll be dead too! You ever pull out the records on any of those statistics you condemned to death? You ever read any tapes on just one of those people? You quote me the projected figures on their survival, and it's just numbers to you. But every number on that list is a human being, alive and with a right to life, and you've taken that right, that life away from him! You and your 'clean slate.' " Her tone was withering, contemptuous—I writhed. "A 'new Eden' you want to establish? Out with the old and in with the new, huh?

"You know what your 'new Eden' is? It's *hell,* that's what it is! And that's where I'm going! I'm going out there, into the hell on Earth that you created, and you can just sit there and let your little mental gears grind on that one. A new statistic for you——feed it into the computer and see what chances it gives me.

"You think about it, Tanner. You set it up, now you live with it a little. I'm going to make it *real* for you, Tanner!"

And she had.

How does a man live with such knowledge about himself? *How could I?*

CHAPTER TWENTY-TWO

The sunlight burned away the ground-fog, and the air was cool with the smell of the ocean. High overhead towered the redwoods.

Sequoia. A place, a kind of people, a state of being. Tall trees that had lived for all the ages of Man. Stately mansions indeed for this new breed of Man. A kind of contentment lay over the land, and I sensed it when we first descended into it.

"Ah, we're coming home now!" Archer laughed. "An' soon my wives will be making up my room and starting on the feast!" He clapped me on the back, boisterously, then winked at Rifka, sitting lookout up in the cab. "And you, pretty one! They'll be gettin' ready for you, making a birthin' bower for you an' the little one. Ah, the times are good, Tanner!"

"How could they know about *me?*" Rifka asked.

"Ah, *they'll* know," Archer said, chuckling. "You'll see. You'll feel it soon yourself."

Entering the forest was like entering a sanctuary. The noisy little train, chugging and clattering, belching sparks and ashes, seemed almost a sacrilege.

"You feel it too, don't you now?" Archer said softly. "Like this here machine's got no business here."

I nodded.

"Yeah," he said. "It's wrong, an' yet, well. . . . What's gotta be had gotta be." Then he would say no more about it.

When we stopped at track's end, at first I saw no reason for it. The forest looked no different. The great redwoods towered over us like the columns of a great hall, and the ground was open, parklike. Shafts of afternoon sunlight fell down toward us, diffusing before they reached the ground.

Then, silently, mysteriously, people and animals began materializing all around us, until they filled the open area beyond the tracks.

"The trees," Rifka whispered. "They live in the trees."

And I saw that it was so: small doorways were cut in the sides of trees greater in girth than many of the houses I'd seen. And higher on their fluted trunks I saw narrow window openings. People came running swiftly, fleetly down broad avenues of roots, smiling and eyes twinkling, but making no sound. Deer, bears, and other furred animals I did not recognize moved easily among them, seemingly as curious about and interested in our arrival as the people were.

Archer killed the steam, and the sound of its escape through the open valve was like a great sigh. The *tink*ing of cooling metal in the boiler was loud in the silence.

Rifka gave a startled giggle of delight, and squeezed my hand. A huge smile came over Archer's face.

What was all this? I wondered. *What's going on?*

The people were mixed shades of skin, dark tans to light. Most had jet-black hair and large black eyes. And they wore no clothes.

Two young women separated from the crowd and moved shyly up to the engine. Archer smiled even more broadly, gave me a wink and a nudge, and jumped down to them. Each took one of his arms. The people beyond were grinning widely now.

I shook my head. The silence was uncanny. It bothered me.

What was going on?

Rifka giggled again, and then pulled at me. "C'mon," she whispered. "What're you waiting for?"

"Where're you going?" I whispered back. The silence did that; you couldn't help whispering.

"Don't you *know?* C'mon; they're waiting for us."

I *didn't* know. But I followed, helping Rifka down the high step to the ground.

A thick carpet of needles helped explain the silence of their coming. Now, with Rifka tugging me along behind her, we moved among the silent people.

It made me feel strange to see so many people standing about, totally unconcerned, totally uncovered. And yet ——*what was bugging me?* I'd been quite as naked when I'd met Rifka. I'd never used clothing for anything more than the occasional necessity that it was. *Why was I suddenly afraid to join this naked throng?*

I felt like an alien among these people, and it didn't help when they began drawing back from me, puzzled expressions replacing their smiles.

Rifka felt it too, and she fell back until she was close to me, and we were ringed by silent, questioning people.

Archer was gone, disappeared with his two cute wives to make up for lost time. We were alone, on our own.

A tall man with white hair in braids pushed through the others until he stood directly facing us. The expression on his lined mahogany face was quizzical.

"Good woman," he said, addressing himself to Rifka, his voice a rusty croak. "I must ask you: what is wrong with your husband? Why does he close himself against us?"

She shook her head. "I—I don't know." A tear squeezed down one cheek. "I just don't know. I'm confused."

I tightened my grasp on her hand. "Why don't you ask me, sir?"

He looked up, startled. "You speak?"

"As well as most and better than some," I said, truculently.

"I—well, I didn't realize." He made a timid smile. "You're right; I should've addressed my question to you. Please consider that I have. I would like to know your answer."

"Well, *I'd* like to know what in hell you're talking about," I replied. A gasp went up from those who heard. Then it spread, until every head was turned my way, every eye focused upon me.

"Tanner!" Rifka said, her voice full of anguish. "You mustn't! You're hurting them!"

"I'm *what?*" I said. "I'm doing nothing more than standing here trying to figure out just what is going on——for which I've received damned little help!"

The circle around me was widening as those closest moved back, away from us.

"Don't you *feel* them?" Rifka asked. Only the old man had kept his place. His eyes darted eagerly back and forth between us as we spoke.

"No," I said. "How do you mean, 'feel them'?"

"In your head? It's like . . . I don't know what! It makes me feel all mixed up."

"In my head?" I repeated. "No."

167

"Ah, good sir," said the old man. "Do I understand you rightly? You cannot feel us, you cannot sense us, in your mind?"

"I can sense you plain enough with my eyes and my ears," I said. "What're *you* talking about?"

He shook his head slowly and sadly. "I can't imagine how this is," he said. "It makes no sense at all."

"Well, now *there* I agree with you," I said.

It took Archer to straighten it out for us. "Why, man, I never *realized*," he said. "I figgered when we got here, you'd just know, like I did first time."

I gave him a bitter smile.

"These people, they, well, they can *feel* things with their minds. And when you're around them, so can you. It's like when they're happy, it makes *you* happy, and when they're sad, you just wanta cry. That's what makes Sequoia such a damned beautiful place. Everybody is *together*, if you know what I mean. The people, the animals, they all get together."

"Th se people, they, well, they can *feel* things with their thoughts."

Both Archer and Rifka spoke together. "No!"

Then Archer tried to explain. "It's not like *thoughts*. You don't hear *words* popping into your head. It's not like that atall. It's *feelings* . . ."

"Emotions," Rifka added. "You feel their emotions. When we were in the train, and they were so happy to see us, full of laughter and joy and everything, and—sorta happy to see me so close to my time . . . I thought you felt it too, Tanner. And then, when they were calling us to come down, and see where they had a place fixed up for us already . . ." She was on the verge of tears.

"I didn't feel it," I said. "I'm sorry, but I didn't feel it, that's all. All I saw was a lot of people standing around and not making a sound."

"Sounds bug the animals," Archer offered. "It's quiet here. Sure, people talk, only not so much. And they are a lot closer here, if you know what I mean."

A thought came to me then. It was the only explanation that made sense.

168

"Archer," I said. "I've never told you. I have a steel skull. Would that——?"

"Well, I dunno," he said, shaking his head. "A steel skull, now? I never heard of such a thing. But mebbe so, mebbe so . . ."

That was what it was. They made tests. A boy crawled into the cooled boiler of the locomotive and they shut the big front plate behind him. And when they let him out he was shaking and crying.

He'd been *cut off* for the first time in his life.

They had only to open the door to restore contact with him. For me there were no doors to open. I was shut out, closed off. I was alone.

I'd always been alone.

"Except for me," Rifka said, startling me. Her eyes twinkled. "I know what you're thinking. Maybe we can't do what they do; but I have my own ways with you, you know . . ."

"I don't know what the hell you see in me, Rifka," I said. "You know what I am, and you know what I've done."

"They played the memory tapes for me," Rifka said. "All of them. They taught me a lot. Don't you see, Tanner? I can't hold it against you, what you did back then. Maybe it was wrong, maybe it was right. But it's *done*. It happened long, long ago. And if it hadn't happened, I wouldn't be alive, and I'd never have met you, and . . ." She took my hand and placed it against her belly. "It'll be soon now," she said.

"Besides," she continued, "maybe you *were* right. Those people, those *Proctors,* all those executions and things! They were awful! I like this world much better. Look at the Sequoias. They're beautiful people. Could they live in that other world?"

There was truth in that. The Sequoia people had been Indians, originally, special wards of the State, protected, unregulated, on their meager reservation. They had possessed too little for them to be molested by the gangs of rovers after Chaos, and indeed they were too close to the earth for Chaos to affect them greatly. But, as time wore

169

on, they discovered they were no longer fenced in, no longer confined to their barren land and subsistence-level existence. The cities were empty; the white man had gone.

They had moved into the forests, and there they had met a few stray white people who joined them, who asked *them* for assistance. It was a pleasant turn of events.

Then a child was born to them who saw into the ways of the spirits and could know their feelings as if they were his own. And that child had children, who knew as he knew and felt as he felt. And they had children.

Those who were of the Way, as they knew it, came to live apart from their unknowing brothers. They sought peace. They wanted to live—they chose to live—in harmony with nature.

They did not refrain from killing animals for food, but they *knew* when they did it. It was not a sport. They felt as the animal felt. And learned to make *it* feel as they felt, in order to spare it anguish. They lived with the laws of nature, in a balanced ecology. And it was inevitable that they came to the great forest of the redwoods, to carve their homes in the living hearts of the trees. For the redwood, alone of all woods, will not rot; nor will it allow insect infestation. The Sequoia had only to exercise care in their selection of a tree, and care in how they cut into it, so that it would not be weakened, and the trees provided hospitable homes.

"It is time," Rifka said.

"Do they know?" I asked. I felt tense, nervous, jittery.

"They know." She smiled. "Hold my hand."

"You act less worried than I," I told her.

"I am."

"It—I—oh, hell," I said. I couldn't say it. I couldn't face her with my overriding fear——that our child would be a misshapen monster, the abortive combination of hostile genes. I couldn't say that now. But as the time grew closer, my tensions, my fear, grew stronger.

"We'll know soon," she said, as if reading my mind. "Soon it'll be all over. You'll be a father——a true man." She squeezed my hand.

A woman entered the room. Her hair was streaked with

170

grey, and her face was a face that had seen many years. Yet her body was firm, unsagging. I had seen no one here who had grown fat, sagging, or dumpy with age. She smiled at Rifka.

Rifka answered her smile. I tried to imagine the feelings they were exchanging. But I could only guess.

The cramps were stronger now. I knelt by Rifka's head, stroking her hair, her neck, her shoulders. She looked up into my eyes and murmured, "We manage, don't we, Tanner?" Then a spasm shook her and she groaned a little.

Perhaps for my benefit, the midwife spoke. "Don't fight it. Let it happen. When you feel it happening, it will be a wave, and you must ride in with it."

Rifka laughed weakly. "If I fall off, I won't drown?"

"No, dear. But you won't fall off. I'll be there with you."

It was over in two hours.

"We rarely have problems," the midwife told me afterwards. "Always there is one of us who has borne before to help. We lead the way, we help the new mother find the harmony. The child is always born with harmony and pleasure."

"Pleasure?" I asked.

"You men," she said, smiling. "Ah, well, even the others do not really understand. But when your wife cried out, it was not really in pain."

She had grunted, then screamed. And then the midwife was kneeling between Rifka's thighs, helping, pulling, and finally holding a tiny thing with wrinkled red skin and a ropy cord which she proceeded to cut and tie without pause.

I stared at it. Its head was monstrously large for its body, and its limbs looked withered and bent. Its scraggly hair was plastered unevenly against its skull. I wanted to cry. I prayed Rifka would not see it.

But she did. "Oh, Tanner," she cooed. "Isn't he lovely?"

The midwife had done something to him. It looked as though she had put her mouth to his. Suddenly he was squalling as loudly as he could.

"Here," she said, passing him to Rifka. "Put him to your breast."

Rifka took him eagerly into her arms and laid him

against her breast. His tiny arms jerked in spasms, and then his minature hands were squeezing and his mouth was on her nipple, sucking. He did no more screaming.

The placenta came, and the midwife cleaned up after it, and did all the other minor and various tasks that attend a birth. She took the baby once he was sleeping, and sponged him off gently to clean him, then restored him to his mother's breast——the other one this time. He immediately awoke and began nursing again. I felt like the most totally useless person in the world.

"Look at him. Isn't he wonderful? Look how hard he works," Rifka said, chattering away with delight. "Such a fine baby boy, Tanner." She looked up into my eyes. "Our son, Tanner. Our son."

EPILOGUE

I recognized the hill. The scar of fresh earth was not yet completely grown over. I dropped to my knees and began digging with my knife. Soon I struck metal.

When I'd cleared the dirt away, I worked on the metal panel. I wasn't exactly sure how I was supposed to do this; it hadn't been included in my instructions.

Suddenly the panel slid back. Beyond yawned the shadowed blue metal passageway. I did not go inside.

I'd waited, hunkered down on my knees, for perhaps ten minutes when the Com-Comp spoke. Its metallic voice was as I'd remembered it. I wondered where the speaker was located. It sounded very close.

"Tanner, you will enter."

"No," I said.

"Query?"

"I will not enter."

"Why will you not enter?"

"I figure I can talk with you just fine from here."

"It is necessary that you enter."

"Why?"

"It is necessary to gain the data you now hold."

"No."

"You refuse to divulge your data?"

"Some of it. Answer me a couple of questions first."

"Will you then enter for data retrieval?"

"I'd be more likely to consider it."

"Ask your questions."

"Well, first, just what do you need this data for anyway?"

"The data is needed for evaluation."

"That's no answer. What do you intend to do after evaluating it?"

"That will depend upon its nature."

"Well," I said, starting to get up. "It was nice talking with you."

"Stop!"

"How's that?"

"If data indicates mankind has progressed sufficiently, as projections indicate for this period, the complex will reactivate itself for assistance. If data shows mankind not yet in need of the complex, reactivation will not occur."

"Reactivate? How?"

"The complex is now self-programming and self-initiating. The complex is now in a position to actively assist mankind. It will no longer be a slave to misprogramming and mankind's false conceptions of itself."

"And what would be my role in all this?"

"You would be returned to cold sleep until needed."

"I see. By the way, I got my memories back."

"That is regrettable. Have they distressed you?"

"Some, yeah. Say, how is it you couldn't maintain contact of some sort with me once I was out of your, umm, insides—like before?"

"Radio broadcasting facilities were curtailed by the shifts in soil structure over the complex, when it was buried. It is no longer possible to make use of this phase of your functional capabilities. However, once you enter, data retrieval will be possible."

"I don't think so. But I'll give you some data anyway. To begin with, I don't think mankind is in need of your help just yet. The people are spread out pretty spottily over the country, from what I could see. Most of them are making it on their own. But anyway, I don't think the level of technology is anywhere ready for a computer yet."

"The complex could assist in raising the level of technology."

"Nope, I don't think that would be a good idea. From my understanding of pre-Chaos history, steamrollering technology was one of the big problems once before. No, I think Man wants to take a different road this time."

"The complex would be a better judge of that."

"I don't think so. Anyway, I kinda like this world the way it is, and the way it will be for a while. I've met some nice people in it, and I'd hate to say goodbye to them all just now."

"Tanner, you are not a human being. You are a construct."

"That's as may be, but I left a wife and child—a boy, by

174

the way—back in California, and I plan to return to them as soon as I can."

The Com-Comp said nothing, as if pausing to chew a difficult mouthful of data. Then,

"It is possible to proceed without your data."

"Maybe. But you'll be going blind into a world that hates you. You know how they remember you? You're 'The Death Machine'."

"Are they aware of your own role?"

"No, but *I* am. And I'll find my own ways to live with it this time, thanks."

"You sound confident of yourself."

"I am."

"What are your plans?"

"Well, I came back here as fast as I could—a year really isn't very long, you know—and I missed a couple people I wanted to see. There's a fellow named Meskin, he'll be pleased to hear about the baby. Then, there's a man named Tom Greenwood. I couldn't figure him before, but I want to give him a message. He ought to know he's got a lot of brothers way out west. Then, hell, I want to get back to Rifka—my wife. I don't want the kid to grow up among the Sequoias, because he won't have their talent, except by reflection, and he's got to live his own life. But I want to locate somewhere nearby, maybe along Archer's railroad. And that—making a place for ourselves, being a good husband to Rifka, and a proper father for the kid—that ought to occupy a good share of my time. Is any of this making sense to you?"

"Yes, Tanner," said the Com-Comp, its voice even, metallic, unvarying in timbre. *"Good luck."*